COWGIRL CHRISTMAS

DONNA ALWARD

ABOUT COWGIRL CHRISTMAS

He can teach her to cook…but can she teach him to love?

Kelley Hughes is a great rancher but a horrible cook, and this year Christmas dinner is on her shoulders. Good thing Mack Dennison is around, chef and owner of Mack's Kitchen store chain. Mack agrees to give Kelley cooking lessons, but Kelley has a few things to teach Mack, as well. He's never had a real family Christmas, and before long she has him out looking for a Christmas tree and hanging ornaments.

As the holiday season weaves its spell, Kelley and Mack find excuses to spend more time together, and it's not long until their feelings deepen into something profound. But Mack's got his own reasons for holding back his heart. Can he trust that Kelley's feelings are real, and believe in his own Christmas miracle?

PRAISE FOR DONNA ALWARD

Never miss a new release again! Sign up for Donna's newsletter and get GET ME TO THE CHURCH ON TIME for FREE!

Kelley Hughes snapped the cell phone closed as her feet automatically stopped outside the grey brick building. She looked up at the burgundy-colored awning and furrowed her brow. Was it some sort of sign that she stopped, at just this moment, in front of "Mack's Kitchen"? Because she'd just assured her sister Amelia that she had Christmas dinner under control, when the truth was she'd barely given it a thought.

She'd been so preoccupied thinking about Gram and the ranch that the holidays had crept up on her. She'd also realized lately that Amelia put on a brave face, but she was handling a lot on her own, being a single mom and running the business part of the ranch single handedly. Kelley wanted to ease some of the load, so she'd put her foot down and told Amelia that she would look after Christmas dinner so her sister could have a break. She thought now she should have volunteered some other service, because her idea of a fancy meal was a rotisserie chicken from the market and the accompanying side salads in plastic dishes.

Surely there wasn't much to making an actual dinner. You put a turkey in the oven and cooked some vegetables, right?

She bit down on her lip, staring at the green garland and twinkle lights decorating the iron railings of the shop. What had she been thinking? She hadn't even done her shopping yet and she was taking on something more? She looked at her watch; she should get back to the hospital. But there was the small matter of the nonexistent shopping she'd done. A display in the window caught her eye—a cookie making kit, complete with cookie cutters and bright red and green sprinkles. It was just the kind of thing Amelia would love to do with Jesse. Already she was mentally crossing the first gift off her list.

Then there would only be the gifts for Gram and Jesse, and she could get back to the hospital. She didn't like leaving Gram alone for long, despite the older woman's insistence she'd be fine.

Gram kept her spirits up, saying it was only tests, but Kelley had seen fear in Gram's eyes for the first time she could remember. Yes, she would finish here and hurry back.

She opened the door, surprised by the old-fashioned bell above the door that announced her entrance. The next thing she noticed was the smell and she paused. It smelled like every holiday rolled into one. Cinnamon and fruit and something else…baked bread? Her house never smelled like this. Ever. Carols played softly over invisible speakers, adding to the homey, holiday warmth.

This was Mack Dennison's latest store in his "Mack's Kitchen" franchise. After three years of building them from San Diego to Seattle, he'd finally come home to Montana and opened one himself. The Rebel Ridge weekly paper had done a feature on him just last week— the hometown boy who had made his fortune and brought it back to Helena. The sharp, savvy man in the picture hadn't jived with the vague memory she had of him from school. Now instead of the tiny house where he'd grown up in Rebel Ridge, he probably had some fancy condo here in the city. But there was no doubt that his stores were welcoming, homey, and stocked to the teeth with anything a cook could possibly want—and then some.

The walls and shelves were lined with pots, pans, and utensils that looked odd and with funny names. Another section heralded the latest in spices and gourmet combinations, specialty foods and recipe books. And smack dab in the middle was the counter and cash register, and a tall, good-looking man in jeans and a ribbed sweater. It suddenly dawned on her it was Mack. He was speaking to a middle-aged woman while bagging her items. She hadn't actually expected to see him here. After all, he was head of a successful chain of stores. She'd pictured him in a corporate tower some-where. The smile she'd worn at the sound of a favorite carol faded away. If she'd known he'd be working the register…well, she might have reconsidered coming in.

When Mack smiled at his customer, Kelley's stomach

did a flip. It was a good smile, with an even row of teeth and a half-dimple that popped in his cheek. He probably didn't even remember who she was. Somehow, she'd always seemed to fade into the woodwork, and that was fine with her.

"Can I help you?"

She blinked, looked up, and tried very hard to make her polite smile more relaxed. "Hello, Mack."

He hadn't changed much. A little older, but still with that tall, lean build, only slightly filled out now that he was past his teenage years. Dark eyes that met hers, making something tingle down her spine. And a half-crooked smile so infectious that she smiled back. She couldn't help it.

"I'm sorry, have we met?"

Embarrassment flamed in her cheeks and her smile faltered. Of course he wouldn't remember her now if he hadn't even known she'd existed then. "You probably don't remember me. I'm Kelley Hughes. I was in your eleventh-grade math class."

His smile dimmed the slightest bit and she wondered why, but just like that it was back up to its normal wattage and she wondered if the glimmer had actually happened at all.

"Of course. I remember now. Kelley Hughes. Your family runs the Rocking H." He held out his hand.

She was sure he was being polite. After a long pause, she held out her hand and let him shake it. The little flutters happened again, quite unexpectedly. He held it a little longer than she'd anticipated, and she pulled her fingers out of his.

"It's been a while," she said quietly. She put her hands in her pockets when she didn't know what else to do with them. Her ability to make small talk seemed to have fled as well. She'd tried to leave high school behind for the most part, certainly shunning parties and well-intentioned get togethers. She and Mack had never run in the same circles, anyway. She had been busy taking over after Grandpa died and he'd disappeared to build his empire, traveling the world. They might both be in Montana again now, but they were miles apart.

He shifted his weight at the long lull in conversation. "So…what are you up to these days? What brings you from Rebel Ridge into Helena?"

He was more adept at chit chat than she was, that much was clear. She chanced a look up into his eyes and for a moment she was caught there. There was some-thing…a tiny flash.

He put a hand on her arm, and she felt the warmth through her heavy jacket, none of the desire to pull away like she expected. But before she could think too much about it, he continued. "I heard about your grandfather's passing. I'm so sorry. How is Mrs. Hughes?"

His inquiry surprised her. Small towns were just that, and in a place like Rebel Ridge everyone tended to hear everyone else's gossip. She was sure he was just being polite again. But the concern touched her nevertheless. Especially now.

Her throat thickened with emotion she'd held in all day.

She moved away, under the pretense of examining

the wares on the shelves nearby. It wasn't that she didn't love the ranch, she did. And right now it was more important to her than ever. But in the back of her mind there was something else that she couldn't shake. There'd never been a question, never been an opportunity for more. She'd worked hard, had looked after things. But there had been places she'd wanted to see. Things she'd wanted to do. Mack had left Rebel Ridge behind and had gone on to build his own business. He'd had a choice.

But more than that, responsibility weighed even heavier on her these days. The whole trip to Helena was for Gram's angioplasty at the hospital, and it was a stark reminder that things were changing.

"Gram's doing fine." She felt a slight twinge at glossing over the truth, but what did it matter? It wasn't like she'd see Mack again. She rarely came into town. She was only here for the week because they hadn't wanted to leave Gram alone. And Mack was busy, now that he'd become somewhat of a local celebrity. She was sure his life here in Helena was busier than it had ever been when they'd both lived in "the Ridge". She was only here to shop.

A pause settled over the pair once more. As the silence drew out, she tried to ignore the way his jeans hugged his body, the breadth of his shoulders, or the fluttering that kept happening in her tummy. It was unfamiliar and she didn't like it. The glimmer of attraction was as foreign to her as the merchandise he carried.

Kelley pasted another smile on for the mere sake of

manners. "I really came in to find a Christmas present for my sister."

Mack's shoulders relaxed. "What did you have in mind?"

"I saw that cookie kit in the window. I'm sure she'd enjoy something like that with her son."

He went to a shelf and pulled out one of the kits she'd seen. Cookies cutters in the shapes of snowflakes, trees, and snowmen danced beneath the plastic coating. Sprinkles and gumdrops were in tiny packages for decorating.

It was exactly the sort of thing Amelia would love. Kelley could give it to her early, and Amelia and Jesse would mix up dough and have a wonderful time cutting out shapes and decorating them for the holidays. The thought put a little ache in her chest. Jesse was such a blessing and a bright spot.

Kelley reached out and took the kit from Mack's hands, running a finger down the jar of red crystallized sugar. Amelia was a wonderful mom, but Jesse wanted a dad. He'd started school this year and was suddenly noticing things. And he'd whispered to Kelley the other day that he'd wished for a dad for Christmas. It had touched her, made her wistful. She let him help out on the ranch, showed him things. But she was Aunt Kelley, not a father. It wasn't anywhere near the same.

"It's perfect," she murmured. "Amelia and Jesse will have a wonderful time." Jesse was so worried about his great-grandmother. Maybe this would help fill in the gaps that couldn't truly be filled. Gaps that she herself had been noticing more lately, in herself. Resentments that bubbled up from nowhere. Longings—the female kind—that had no place as foreman of a ranch. A need to be more than that somehow. And not know how—or if—she should begin.

But there was no time for those thoughts now. She had her hands full with Rocking H and looking after Amelia and Ruby. It had always been that way and wasn't likely to change any time soon.

She looked up at him, unprepared for the expression mirrored back at her.

His dark eyes were soft with what might have been understanding, his lips unsmiling. "Yes," he said quietly. "Kids like baking and decorating. And Mrs. Hughes too, I expect."

"She probably won't be up to it after…"

Kelley broke off, realized that she'd said too much as his brows pulled together.

"After what?" The spell that had been tenuously woven around them dissipated. She averted her eyes.

"Nothing."

But he'd already picked up on the hesitation in her voice. "Is there something wrong? You sound upset."

"She is…she will be. It's nothing."

And yet it was. Somehow talking in riddles to Mack brought emotions to the surface and she swallowed, trying to beat them back. Gram was the glue. She and Grandpa had raised her and Amelia after the death of their parents and then Gram had kept the ranch going after his death several years ago. Kelley had stepped in as she knew she eventually would, but it was Gram who was the heart and soul of the Hughes clan and her illness made Kelley suddenly realize there might not be that many more Christmases with them all together. She blinked and picked up a package that read Chili Pickled Pears. The label blurred.

"Kelley."

She looked up in alarm. The way he said her name sounded somewhere between a command and an endearment. It was silly considering she hadn't seen him for nearly a decade. He'd been busy making his way in the world and she'd stayed in exactly the same place where they'd grown up. But in his eyes was a gentle invitation and she found herself revealing more than she'd planned.

"I'm in Helena because Gram's in the hospital," she explained, her throat tightening once more.

"Is it serious?"

"She's had some tests, and she's scheduled for an angioplasty tomorrow."

Mack placed a hand on her arm and she felt the warmth soak through her jacket and sleeve, right to her skin. Rather than repelling, it was comforting. "I hadn't heard."

"It isn't exactly community knowledge. She wanted to keep it quiet. The doctors say she'll be fine, but…"

"It's a bit scary," he finished.

"Yes," she admitted. She hadn't spoken to anyone about her fears about Gram. Mack was the very first person who seemed to care about how *she* might be feeling and for that reason alone, she found herself responding to his gentle comments.

For some strange reason she thought it might be nice

to be comforted in his arms. But that was insane. She didn't do physical touches. And she wasn't sure she'd know how to accept comfort anyway. Her own two feet was how she normally dealt with things. She didn't rely on other people. Perhaps that was why the thought of losing Gram panicked her so much. Gram was the one person Kelley had *always* counted on.

She cleared her throat. "Anyway," she continued, "with my nephew Jesse in school, Amelia couldn't really come, and we didn't want to leave Gram here alone. So I'm staying at a motel near the hospital until it's over and I can take her home."

"I'm sorry, Kelley. This must be difficult, especially so close to the holiday." His fingers squeezed, reassuring. "If there's anything I can do to help…everyone in Rebel Ridge knows and loves Mrs. Hughes."

Yes, everyone loved Ruby. And Amelia. If Kelley didn't hold the family together, who would? But then what was left for her? It was a heavy load, trying to be all things for all people.

The afternoon was waning and she still had to pick up other gifts. "I should get going," she said, hiding a sigh and taking her purchase up to the cash register. "I need to finish up my shopping and get back to the hospital. And the forecast said there's a storm coming."

"When did you eat last, Kelley?"

She met his gaze, a bit confused at his concern. "Me? Why?"

"Because you look a little pale. And like you could use a bite. Here, try this." He plucked a small square from a silver tray and held it in front of her mouth.

She looked at his hand warily, holding out some sort of sweet. It smelled wonderful, spicy and rich. She swallowed, but her mouth watered anyway, and her tummy rumbled the slightest bit. She shifted her gaze to his face and he raised one eyebrow.

She opened her mouth, and he popped the morsel into it.

Mmmm. Chewy, moist, rich, and spicy. She closed her eyes. Just this one bite was far better than anything she'd had at the hospital cafeteria today. Or any day this week, since that was where she'd had most of her meals.

"What *is* that?"

With a self-satisfied smile, he picked up her package of pickled pears. "Fruitcake."

But she hated fruitcake. Normally.

"Try what's on the other tray."

She reached over and picked up an odd-looking, golden-brown packet. The cube of fruitcake had only increased her hunger and she took a substantial bite. Flavor exploded on her tongue…pastry and butter and…was that ham? Something tasted like dill. She ate the rest without hesitation. "That's really good, Mack." The compliment didn't hurt as much as she'd expected it would. She offered her first, unfettered, genuine smile. "Not bad for a boy from the Ridge."

"I can share the recipe if you like."

Once again, she felt awkward and her smile wavered. She was no domestic goddess and most of the time felt no need to apologize for it. But lately she'd had stirrings…a vague sense of dissatisfaction that while she was great at running the ranch, as a woman she was a bit of a failure. And then a resulting anger at herself because that was ridiculous. Being able to cook and sew and do all those things Amelia was a natural at didn't make her less of a woman.

No, the reasons went far deeper than that, in scars that would never completely go away.

"I could take it for Amelia." She didn't want to admit she couldn't even make boxed macaroni and cheese. "I'm in charge of the ranch. Amelia runs the house." She smiled politely. "We play to our strengths." The fact that her sister was the nurturer of all of them —including being a fantastic single parent, made Kelley proud.

"So you don't cook...at all?"

The surprised tone of his voice took any shred of femininity she'd had and thrown it out the window. She was suddenly aware of what she was wearing—faded jeans and a serviceable, sexless jacket. Even her scarf now seemed a dull shade of brown. Grandpa had often teased that she was his "boy" and at one time it had made her proud. She'd loved being by his side, working with the livestock. But then she'd had glimpses of her own dreams that were brought to a sharp end when he was gone and it was up to her to keep the ranch going for Amelia and Grandma Ruby. Lord knew Ruby was still the head of the family, but she wasn't up to the task of the physical running of the ranch. That was left to Kelley. She'd known her duty to her family and had done it.

But his surprise at her lack of culinary skills made her bristle. "Actually, I'm cooking the family Christmas dinner this year." Up went her chin again. She'd be damned if she'd let him know that the extent of her cooking was frying a plain old egg for breakfast or putting together a sandwich. She grew suddenly inspired. "As a matter of fact, while I'm here I can look for some new and interesting ideas to add to the meal."

New and interesting, indeed. She knew nothing about putting on a dinner, but she was sure she could do it. She'd never failed at anything she'd tried before. It only took diligence and hard work, like any other difficult task.

"Oh, that's a shame then. I was thinking you should come take a class. I run them through the week, for all sorts of people. Men and women, young and old. We start with boiling water. It's a bird course; impossible to fail. But if you're interested in ideas…"

A cooking school? She hadn't taken home ec the first time and she sure didn't want to do it now. Besides, remembering high school was a huge source of pain for her. She'd rather just leave it all behind. She probably wouldn't even have come in today if she'd known he was going to be here. "I don't have the time for anything elaborate."

She set her teeth. Just because she didn't cook didn't mean she couldn't. She could still hear the skepticism in Amelia's voice when she'd offered to do the dinner on Christmas Eve. Her laugh had been followed by the suggestion of a caterer. It had been good-natured sisterly teasing, but it had stung just the same. Now, looking up in Mack's handsome face, she really felt as though she had something to prove.

"Would what I tasted work as an appetizer? For my Christmas dinner? You did say you had the recipe."

Briefly she imagined bringing out a tray with warm, golden-brown squares, serving perhaps a glass of wine or punch before dinner while Jesse played with his new toys and carols played on the stereo. What would Amelia say then? Amelia had been so determined to look after the ranch work in Kelley's absence. Surely Kelley could prove herself equally adept at Amelia's forte. She was getting so tired of being the sister in jeans and boots. There was more to her than that. Maybe she was finally ready to let someone see it, instead of hiding behind it.

"Absolutely. They're easy as anything."

She highly doubted it, but they couldn't be that hard, could they? "That would be great, Mack. I appreciate it."

He jotted down the recipe on a card and put it in the bag with the rest of her purchases. "You'll need some of my dill seasoning. The rest of the items you can buy at the grocery store."

He put in a bottle and rang in the pears and cookie kit. At the last moment he took a small bag from beneath the counter and tucked it in with her purchases.

"A little treat for Ruby, if you can sneak it in."

"I'll do that." She paid and put the receipt in her wallet.

"Give my best to your family, Kelley."

"I will."

She was nearly to the door, tugging her mittens back over her hands, when she heard his warm voice once more, sending a delicious shiver down her arms.

"And Kelley?"

She half turned to look back at him.

"Merry Christmas."

For some inexplicable reason, the simple wish made the backs of her eyes sting. She pulled on her mitten, gripped the door handle, and stepped out into the bitter cold.

2

"**D**ammit!"

Kelley dropped the pan on to the stove top, fanning away smoke as she sucked on her burned finger.

The puffs were ruined, completely ruined. She took off the oven mitt and went to the window, pushing it open a crack and letting the cold air in and the acrid smell out. She'd picked up the rest of the ingredients on Mack's list and taken them back to the motel thinking a trial run would help her put in some time while the storm blew outside.

Only there'd been a flaw in her plan. The one aluminum baking sheet in the kitchenette cupboard now appeared charred beyond repair. The tops of the phyllo puffs were burned. And several of the pastry sheets lay shredded on the small countertop amid a mess of prosciutto, parmesan, asparagus, and Mack's dill season-ing. The mess was held together by bits of greasy melted butter that hadn't behaved...perhaps because she hadn't had something the recipe called a pastry brush. She'd tried using the curved end of a fork, but it had made nothing but a mess.

She was in deep, deep trouble. She pushed back a few strands of hair that had escaped her braid. The recipe had sounded simple. If she couldn't even make a simple hors d'oeuvre, how could she expect to pull off a whole dinner without burning down the house?

A knock sounded on the motel door as she dumped the whole lot of ruined food in the garbage. "Hello? Everyone okay in there?"

And the pan froze in her hand.

Okay, so she was thinking about Mack, and the way he'd held her hand longer than necessary today. That was the only reason it sounded like his voice outside.

She went to the door and looked out the peep hole. "Oh no," she breathed, pressing her hands to her cheeks and attempting to smooth her wild hair. She looked a fright. It *was* Mack. His dark eyes flashed, his jaw was taut as he lifted his hand to bang on the door again. She jumped at the harsh contact of fist to wood, her heart taking up a frantic hammering.

"Are you okay? I smelled smoke!" She heard the urgent tone of his voice and had the desperate thought he'd do something stupid like call 911 if she didn't answer.

"Hello? Answer me!"

Oh, hell! What if he broke down the door?

"Just a minute," she called, spinning in a frantic circle.

She opened the door, stood firmly in the breach.

Snow swirled around Mack's head as his shoulders hunched against the storm.

"Kelley?"

Busted. "What in the world are you doing here?" she demanded, attempting to look defiant though her pulse was still pounding.

"I smelled smoke and was afraid of a fire." Without a how do you do, he pushed by her and into the room. "Is everything okay?"

"Perfectly fine."

She hated how the words came out with a quaver at the end, or how his bursting past her sent a spiral of fear from her head to the tip of her toes. Alone, in a motel room, with a man she didn't exactly know. Memories rushed back, sharp as knives and she beat them aside angrily. She was sick to death of men—and her memories—having all the power.

"Is that awful smell asparagus puffs?"

Humiliation made her want to sink through the floor, and she had the thought that at least it would provide an escape route. She instinctively shuffled sideways so that she had the door directly behind her. "It was. Definitely past tense."

He coughed. "What did you cook them with, a blow torch? At least I know you're all right and not setting the entire motel on fire."

His obvious concern alleviated a bit of panic she'd inevitably felt at his bursting in. "What in the world are you doing here!"

He shook his head, sending snowflakes sprinkling off

his hair. "I'm staying next door. Until my house is finished."

"Your house?" What was he talking about? He was living here? And building a house?

"You didn't know?"

She shook her head. "No."

"I thought the people in Rebel Ridge kept the grapevine going better. Mabel Reese must be slacking. I'm building a house out on the bluff."

She refused to be charmed by his reference to the town gossip who kept everyone in the know whether they wanted to be or not. "And you're here…" She went to close the window and left the idea hanging, still aware that if it came to it, she could reach the doorway first.

He smiled, popping the one dimple most unfairly. "You mentioned a motel in the shop today. I had no idea it was this one. Small world, huh?"

Too small to her mind.

He wrinkled his nose, raked his gaze over her dough-studded clothing, and merely said, "Oh boy."

And yet it suddenly dawned on her that before her stood a man who was capable of helping her with her dilemma. Just not tonight. Not in a motel room. Her blood momentarily seemed to run cold. If she could just ask him, and get rid of him, it would be fine. If he agreed, they'd meet somewhere she felt safe. A controlled environment, like his school. One with lots of people around.

· · ·

Mack looked around him. Mess was everywhere. The bed was the only untouched area in the room. Kelley Hughes, class wallflower, stood before him in old jeans spotted with what looked like dough and spots of grease. Her hair was coming out of her braid and her cheeks were flushed. She had a hard time meeting his eyes.

Everything about her made his blood leap. She was beautiful this way, less than perfect. Without the cool control she had exhibited this afternoon, though she was trying hard, he could tell. He hadn't remembered her at first, not until she'd said her name and he remembered the quiet girl who'd sat at the back of his math class. She'd been the studious type, and he'd been too withdrawn to say anything to her anyway.

The acrid smell was horrible, but he teased out bits of what was likely pastry and ham. He hid a smile. He'd been correct on the first guess...asparagus puffs. Nothing was burning down. It was just burned.

Her soft voice interrupted his analysis. "I'm afraid the puffs didn't turn out as I expected."

"What happened?"

She looked like she was about to swallow a canary. Despite her words this afternoon, he'd bet his boots she couldn't cook. Someone who could, wouldn't have looked so uncomfortable surrounded by pots and utensils.

She took a deep breath. "I can't cook. Not a bit."

"No kidding." A grin tugged the corner of his mouth as her eyes narrowed.

"Look, save the smart remarks, okay? I promised

everyone a Christmas dinner…I can't ask my sister to put more on her plate. She's looking after the ranch right now while I'm gone, and there's her son Jesse, and she's going to have Gram when she comes home…" She broke off, took a breath. "But you have a cooking school. You could help."

Well, well. She was asking for help after all. It surprised him.

"Yes, lessons are once a week, above the store."

Snow melted off his dark hair, trickling in a cold path down the back of his neck. He saw the glimmer of despair in her eyes. His regular cooking classes wouldn't cut it, not with the tight timing, and they both knew it. "But Christmas is in days, not weeks," he added.

"I'm aware of that." She sighed. But there was something else behind it, and he wasn't sure what. She looked like at this moment she'd like to be somewhere else. Anywhere else.

"Do you want *me* to cook dinner for your family?"

It was only dinner. Surely it didn't matter that much who cooked it. What mattered was being together, or so he was told.

Kelley folded her hands in front of her, and he saw the red tip on her index finger—she'd burned herself.

"That would be the easy way, I suppose. But no thank you. I need to do this myself." She jutted her chin. "Right now, you're the only one I can think of to help me. I want you to show me, Mack. I need to do this. I need to prove to them I can do it." She turned her hazel eyes up to him, fringed with dark lashes. "I need to prove it to myself."

He swallowed against the rush of something he didn't want to acknowledge. Someone needed him. And that was a rarity.

"Will you teach me how to make a Christmas dinner for my family?"

Mack fought back the sudden urge to hug her. The woman standing before him now thought she looked tough, he was sure of it. She obviously cared deeply about her family—that scored points with him.

Her imploring eyes were exactly the sort of reason he'd started Mack's Kitchen in the first place. And maybe helping her would make Christmas something to look forward to this year, take away the monotony of the holiday. Help him to forget why he'd never bought into the whole Christmas magic thing. The one time he had...it had been a disaster.

Holiday cheer wasn't for him, but he understood the need for it in other people. Why else had he opened Mack's Kitchen anyway? "I'll help you."

"You will?"

He chuckled at the astonishment he heard in her voice. "Yes, I will. Teaching is what I do, and from what you've said, no one else in your family is up to it. Besides..." he looked around him at the mess, then slid his gaze back to hers. "I do enjoy a challenge."

"Ha ha."

"And since I can't see us making it out for any groceries right now, how much phyllo have you got left? We might as well get started."

.   .   .

"Here?" Kelley's eyes darted from him to the door and back, her jumbled up nerves suddenly back with a vengeance. She'd meant at his store. At his place of business. Not a motel room in the middle of the night! "I don't think that's a good idea."

"Are you expecting someone?" he asked.

The worldly question sent a blush straight up her neck. "No! Of course not!" Her eyes widened further as his dimple popped again and she realized he was teasing. There wasn't much time before Christmas and a lot of work to do. But a motel room?

"Come on, this is much more fun than being stuck in with only the television for company. Besides, you fall off the horse, you get right back on. It can't be that bad."

She followed him into the kitchen and she realized how it must look to him. It was a complete disaster.

He grinned and that damnable dimple popped. "Okay, so I was wrong. It can be that bad." A laugh rippled up and out of his throat. "Sit tight. I'm going to pop back next door for a minute." He made it to the door and looked back. "And Kelley? Don't touch anything."

Moments later he was back carrying his own kitchenette-stocked sheet, a half head of broccoli, a packet of eggs, cheese, and a tiny spice bottle.

"What's all that?"

"Dinner."

Kelley hadn't followed his instructions to the letter, but she'd cleaned a tidy space on the counter. He put the sheet on the stove top and rubbed his hands together. "Okay," he said. "First the pastry."

Kelley stood several feet away as he went to get the phyllo. He had no idea how uncomfortable she was right now, and she'd cut off her own arm before she'd explain. In her head she knew the quiet boy she remembered was harmless. But her subconscious kept shouting something else. She wasn't used to being railroaded, and he'd burst in tonight and taken over. But she was the foreman of a ranch. She could do this.

"Kelley, you can't cook from over there." He beckoned her over. She swallowed and quietly went to his side. Gently he showed her how to separate the sheets and lay them out carefully. "Where's your pastry brush?"

"I haven't got one."

He muttered an exclamation and picked up the bowl of melted butter. "That's why it looks so torn, then. We'll have to improvise."

He turned his head to look at her and she shrugged. "Improvise."

He laughed at her simple response. "You know."

She still didn't get his meaning. Improvise what?

"Okay, so you don't know. Let's put it in ranch terms. Imagine there's a fence line broken, and you left your tools somewhere. What do you do?"

"You're going to equate pastry with fences." The analogy relaxed her and she leaned forward, watching the motion of his hands.

"Don't be so narrow-minded. Look. We use our fingers instead. Come here. Dip and spread." She put her hands on the dough and he quickly reached out to stop her. "Gently," he said quietly, holding her hand in his and guiding it, smoothing the butter on the phyllo.

Kelley's stomach clenched, full of nerves. His hands were firm and sure on hers, the slick texture of the butter warm beneath their fingertips as they smoothed it over the fragile sheets. His body nestled close behind her; she felt the strong heat of it against her back as he guided her hands. Never in the last decade had she let a man get this close to her. There'd never been a need for personal contact at Rocking H.

She was sure he couldn't tell the battle waging within her—the thin, sharp thread of fear warring with a shocking need to feel close to him. Or her surprise at realizing she wanted to feel close to him. This afternoon his quiet concern had been genuine, and something told her that she was safe.

She chanced a look up at him. Big mistake. For in the moment she turned her head to look up, he looked down, and their gazes caught. His pupils were dark. Not teasing at all, but open and curious, like he was trying to see right down into the core of her. She hadn't expected this at all...not Mack, not cooking, and certainly not the knot of awareness that was settling low within her.

There was something here. She caught her lip between her teeth and worried it. Right now they had their hands in butter and dough and all she could think was how good looking he was, the way he had tiny crinkles at the corners of his eyes or how broad his shoulders were as she was snuggled between them.

She bit down on her lip, fighting back the instinctive

fear that rose up without warning.

"What's next?" She made herself say something to break the silence.

A slow smile curled his lips and Kelley felt completely out of her depths. She hadn't meant it as an innuendo of any sort, but what else would he think as she stood there staring at him like a lovesick kitten? She had to stop this. She wasn't interested in Mack Dennison, or any man for that matter. What she wanted was to bake proscuitto and asparagus puffs.

She kept his gaze but stiffened her shoulders. "I meant with the recipe."

To her amazement the smile grew bigger. "I assumed nothing less."

Kelley huffed and turned away. That was enough of being silly and making calf-eyes. "You've certainly broken out of your shy shell."

"You can't build a business by hiding away in a closet."

She wanted to reach out and give him a push, but then remembered that her fingers were coated in butter. She moved away to the sink where she rinsed and dried her hands, away from his body, feeling safer with distance. "Are you saying you had to force yourself?"

"That's exactly what I'm saying. I don't know if you noticed, but I wasn't the most personable kid in class. I had to learn to meet people. To like people. So I did."

She wished she could shed her old self so easily. She turned away. "I thought you were going to help."

"And so I am. Just having a little fun. Don't you think this should be fun?"

Kelley remembered holding Gram's hand as she lay in the cardiac care unit. And little Jesse's face as he whispered to her what he'd asked for Christmas. All the little resentments faded away in those moments; family was everything. She squared her shoulders.

"I need to do this, Mack, and cooking is beyond me."

"Okay."

She paused, surprised at his easy acceptance. "That's it?" He wasn't going to bait her more, or tease her, or ask her why it was so difficult?

"Don't be so hard on yourself. You run a ranch, for Pete's sake. You can't be expected to do everything well."

"I'm not used to being incapable."

"And I bet it kills you to admit it." He grinned.

She raised an eyebrow and he relented. He touched her again, his hand resting on her shoulder. He'd touched her more today than any man had in a long time. What was odd was that it wasn't accompanied by her usual instinct to run or curl into a ball.

"All teasing aside. Everyone can cook, once they learn how. You've just never learned, that's all." He stepped back and reached for some of the thinly sliced ham. "Then let's cook, Kelley. I promise it won't be all that painful."

When she looked at his warm smile, she knew he was wrong. Because already she was feeling a tightness around her chest that had little to do with cooking.

Together they layered on ham, asparagus, fresh parmesan, and Mack's dill seasoning. He showed her how to fold the pastry over and slice it, laying each piece on his own baking tray. He slid it into the oven and showed her how to work the timer...all without making her feel stupid or inept. All with little touches, correcting her hand or showing her how to slice the rounds without tearing. Touches that she sensed meant nothing to him, and maybe that was why she seemed to accept them. He was in his role of teacher.

When it was done, he found a larger mixing bowl. "Now what are you doing?"

"I'm not. You are. You're going to make us dinner. A few appetizers does not a meal make."

"But I can't..."

He merely raised an eyebrow. "You can. This was one of the first things we learned to make in home ec. Mrs. Farber was a strict one, remember her?"

Kelley turned a potholder over in her fingers. "I never took home ec, remember?"

"Oh right." He seemed oblivious to her discomfort and continued. "She had this saying...a place for everything and everything in its place. She was terrifying. But she knew how to cook, and she knew how to teach it. So tonight, I get to pass the torch."

She angled him a dry look.

"Right, well, maybe no torches."

She couldn't help the smile that trembled on her lips at his joke. "What am I making?"

"Crustless Quiche."

She couldn't help it, she rolled her eyes. "Quiche? Seriously?"

"You can scramble the eggs if you want, but this is

much better and hardly more work. We don't have proper pastry, so we'll go crustless."

A small search revealed one round baking dish. In no time Kelley had whipped eggs, grated cheese, added in bits of broccoli and some of the leftover ham from the asparagus rolls, and a dash of something from a bottle in Mack's hand. It all poured into the buttered pan, ready to go in the oven the moment the appetizers came out.

"I did that."

"Yep." He leaned back against the counter with a satisfied smile as she slid the oven mitt off her hand. The perfectly browned tops of the puffs were on the stove, cooling.

"I have a quiche in the oven."

"Indeed. Usually we don't get to that until lesson two, but you did a great job."

Kelley looked up at him. He'd been a gentleman. He'd been patient and understanding and easy to be around.

"Thank you, Mack."

She didn't know how to put the rest into words without sounding encouraging, so she simply let herself smile and popped one of the fresh bites in her mouth. Delicious. And not a black burn mark on them.

"I forgot. I brought one more thing."

Mack boosted himself away from the counter and went to the fridge. He took out a bottle of white wine and a swiss army knife from his pocket. Within seconds he'd flipped out a corkscrew.

Kelley got two glasses from the cupboard. She could

hardly kick him out after he'd helped her—and provided most of the groceries. The hour they'd spent cooking had gone a long way in gaining a simple, yet tentative trust.

"Tumblers?"

She laughed. "What do I look like, the Waterford factory?"

"They'll do, then. Though to be honest...this is more of a whiskey joint sort of place."

He poured the wine into the glasses as lovely smells came out of the oven. Kelley grabbed a plate and put the asparagus rolls on it, moving to the tiny dropleaf table that was set up in the outer area of the motel room.

"This wasn't the dinner you planned tonight, I bet."

"No."

"How's your grandmother?"

His asking pleased her. "Hanging in there. Her procedure has been postponed though." She was surprised but touched by the concern in his eyes. "Not because of her condition," she added hastily. "The weather warning. The hospital is postponing non-emergent procedures until after the storm."

"And she's going to be fine?"

"The doctor says so. But..."

She stopped as a lump formed in her throat. Grandma Ruby was everything to her and Amelia. She took a sip of wine, unwilling to put voice to her fears.

At her long silence, Mack leaned forward. "Is it worse than you said? Is there more? What's the but?"

"But she has a heart condition, and it has really

made us realize that she's getting older. That she won't be around forever. And so maybe part of this whole Christmas thing is just me wondering how many more Christmases we'll all have together. I don't know what I'd do without her, Mack."

It was an intimate confession, especially between the two of them; two that had always known *of* each other but had never been friends. She didn't know why she was able to talk to him so easily. Maybe because in many ways he was a stranger, and it was easier to admit things when there was that bit of natural distance between them.

Mack reached across the small table and took her hand in his. All she could do was squeeze back.

Kelley stared down at their joined fingers. Mack's thumb rubbed over the top of her hand, the friction creating a warmth she was unused to. Normally she would have pulled away immediately. But this time she accepted the simple touch.

"I'm sure she's going to be fine. Try not to worry so much."

Kelley pulled her hand away. "I'm just out of sorts. I'm not used to being away from the ranch for so long, and Amelia's not answering her cell phone. She probably forgot to charge it."

"I take it that's happened before."

A smile flirted with the edges of her lips. "A time or two."

"So why didn't she bring Ruby into town?"

Kelley took a sip of the wine. She licked the remnants off her lips and sighed. "It's harder for her.

She has Jesse to worry about now, and he's started school. You've seen my cooking." This got a smile. "We'd all starve if it were left to me. I hired an extra hand to help out while I was gone, but I don't know if he arrived before the storm or not. Amelia insisted she could manage. But I just don't know."

"You really don't have much faith in people, do you?"

The quiet question unsettled her. Maybe what had happened to her made her lose faith. She kept to her inner circle—her family—and today's foray into the cooking world with Mack was definitely an aberration. The ding of the oven timer saved her from answering.

She went to take the quiche out while Mack went to the window and parted the curtains, looking out. "It's picked up out there. You can't even see across the street."

Kelley looked over at him, feeling the intimacy grow, unsure what to do about it. Here they were, shut up in a small motel room in the middle of the first real storm of the year. She pushed away the nervousness that suddenly popped up again. She didn't do well in closed spaces. At least the lights were on. "Good thing you're just next door. It's a short commute."

He laughed, the sound warm and masculine. "You wouldn't send me away before dinner, would you?"

She suddenly wanted him to go, but somehow wanted him to stay, too. The thought of being here alone in the blizzard seemed so dismal that she nearly welcomed the company. Normally when a storm was coming, she bunked up at the house with Gram and

Amelia and Jesse. Amelia looked after everyone and Kelley played board games with her nephew. Being stuck in town at a half-rate motel wasn't quite as heart-warming. Somehow having Mack with her made her feel safer, and that was unexpected.

"You helped me make it. I suppose it's unlikely you'll be poisoned."

Again the laugh…my word, he laughed easily, and it sent ripples of pleasure down her arms. Kelley reached up for plates in the tiny cupboard, ignoring the quiver in her belly that his voice ignited. She handed him a plate but he paused with it between their hands.

"Would you like me to be poisoned?"

She looked up into his eyes, bright with teasing. He was having fun with her. And she liked it. The moment held; her breath caught as his smile faded and his gaze dropped to her open lips.

Was he considering kissing her?

Breath came back in with a rush of panic on its heels as she thrust the plate in his hand. "Keep it up and I'll find a way."

He reached into a drawer and pulled out a knife for cutting the quiche. He put it into her hand, his fingers warm over hers as she gripped the handle. He was a touchy one! She shivered as he leaned close to her ear and whispered, "Poison's cleaner, but a knife will do the trick in a pinch."

That was it. She stomped her foot and wheeled. "Stop it, you infernal tease!"

The lights flickered. They looked up at the fixture together, and then everything went dark.

3

"Power's out."

"Thanks, Einstein." She put the knife back on the counter next to the warm quiche and tried to cover her sudden unease. His form was dark, his face shadowed in the dimness. The intimacy of earlier was back, sharp and immediate. She tried to make her heart stop pounding so furiously, make her breaths regular. She put several feet of countertop between them.

Mack was already searching the end table beside the bed for matches and she watched his shadowed form with her heart in her throat. She tried to push the memories away. He was not Wilcox, and this was not an abandoned cabin in the middle of nowhere. This was Mack, in a motel room.

In the dark in the middle of the first big blizzard of the year. Her heart clubbed against her ribs painfully.

"Any luck with matches?"

She jumped at the sound of his voice. "Not yet," she croaked, opening a single drawer with shaking fingers. A part of her wanted to reach out and let him shelter her. And yet the thought also scared her to death. She didn't know him well enough. His caring had drawn her to him tonight, but how well did she really know him? She didn't.

"Do you have a flashlight anywhere?"

His voice sounded huskier in the darkness and she swallowed thickly. "I think there's one in the truck. I can go look."

"In this weather?

"But we can't just sit here in the dark!"

She could tell he was grinning even though she couldn't make out the details of his face.

"Why not? I do some of my best work in the dark."

"Stop smiling. This isn't funny." Indeed it was not. She was torn between fear of being alone and fear of being with him and she was becoming more tied up in knots by the second.

"Okay," he relented. "Look, the meal is cooked." He moved to stand beside her and picked up the knife. "Can you see enough to get some forks? We might as well eat while it's warm."

She nodded, but he caught her hesitancy. "Are you scared of the dark, Kelley?"

A tiny thread of hysteria bubbled inside her. The dark? That and then some. "A little."

"I used to be, too. I was hoping if I made light of it…but it didn't work, did it?" He reached out and kneaded her shoulders and she closed her eyes, focusing on the reassuring sound of his voice and not the horrible memories she kept trying to push away.

"How did you stop?" There was no sound in the room beyond their breathing. And then she held her breath and there was just him.

"I don't know. I guess I just stood up to it." His fingers rubbed the tendons on the side of her neck and she exhaled slowly. "It's okay. You're not alone in here. We've got shelter from the storm and we've even got dinner. You don't need to be afraid."

But she was afraid. "The walls feel small," she whispered, and to her surprise, he rested his chin on the top of her head.

"I know," he said, and her heart squeezed.

He gave her shoulders a final rub and backed away. "Let's have something to eat. Maybe after that the power will be back on."

She found utensils with shaky hands and Mack scooped up servings for both of them. He was taking the plates to the table when a knock sounded at the door, the sharp sound making her jump yet again in the darkness.

"Hello? Miss Hughes?"

Kelley stood and went closer to the door. "Yes?"

"It's Jerry Smith, the owner. I wanted to make sure you're all right."

"I'm fine, thank you," she called through the door, and stepped forward to open it.

"Don't bother opening the door, miss, keep your heat in. There should be an emergency candle in the very bottom drawer beside the stove. Hopefully the power won't be out for long."

"Jerry," Mack called out, "It's Mack. No need to check on me."

Kelley blushed. Smith didn't know her, but Mack was a bit of a celebrity, and here they were in a motel room together. Her cheeks felt like fire and she pressed her cool fingers to them.

"Okay, Mack. I'll carry on. Colder 'n hell out here."

"You know the owner?" Kelley whispered, lowering her hands to her side instead of pressed to her still-warm cheeks.

"I've been here for two months already, remember?"

The chill was already seeping through the walls. "Come on," she suggested. "Let's eat before it gets cold."

Mack found the candle and a simple holder, put it in the middle of the tiny table and poured more wine. She sat stiffly and picked up her fork, ignoring the way the candlelight highlighted his cheekbones, throwing the hollows into shadow. "Let's just eat, and maybe by the time we're done, the lights will be back on." She let out a shaky breath. "I guess Jesse will get his white Christmas after all."

She took a bite of the quiche, surprised at how good it tasted. "It's not bad!"

"I told you anyone can cook." He took a bite of his own.

The candlelight flickered and she lifted her eyes to meet his. "Like you said, it's not turkey and trimmings."

"We'll get you there," he smiled, and she smiled back. For several minutes they made small talk about Rocking

H and how he'd spent his time since seeking his fortune. The candle burned lower and the conversation grew lazy. She talked about Ruby and Amelia and mentioned Jesse's Christmas wish for a father and how it had touched her. The smile faded from his lips and his eyes grew serious.

"So if you could have one Christmas wish, what would it be?"

She opened her mouth to answer but he stopped her, holding up a finger. "Wait. One wish for Kelley. Not for anyone else."

What would she wish for? She had the ranch and Amelia and Gram and Jesse, and she loved them. But lately she had wondered what else was out there, for her. She'd always wanted to travel, see some of the world, meet new people and experience new things. Instead she'd been tied to Rocking H in so many ways. And Mack had just told her how he'd gone and done all those things and had come back, successful, even rich. It made her wish seem foolish.

"More," she whispered finally. "I want more." She suddenly felt unbearably guilty for saying it, knowing she should be thankful for having so much. She pushed out her chair and went to the sink, holding on to the edge.

She heard Mack's chair scrape away from the tiny table. He stepped forward until he was only a breath away. Close enough she could smell him...soap and some sort of manly aftershave, somehow magnified in the semi-darkness.

"Kelley, look at me."

"This is highly unusual." She spoke to the wall behind the sink. "We hardly know each other. I can't imagine why I've said as much as I have. I don't usually…" She hesitated. "Maybe this dinner isn't a good idea anyway. I can cater…" she started to babble. "It really doesn't matter. And I need to get back as soon as possible…"

"Stop." Strong hands gripped her arms and turned her around. "Lord, it was a simple question."

She froze at the feeling of his hands on her arms. After a few seconds his fingers relaxed, and she let out the breath she'd pulled in. Nothing about this evening was simple. Especially not the way he seemed able to knock down fences she'd erected years ago.

"Kelley," he murmured.

She felt like weeping. She'd tried to hide things tonight but apparently, she'd failed. He'd seen clear through her bravado and attempt at coolness. She stared at his chest, focusing on a pewter medal that hung from a chain. "I want to see new places. I want to do things." In the darkness she seemed able to whisper her thoughts like a confession. "I want people to see me as more than the ranch foreman in dusty jeans and dirty boots."

She couldn't look at him, not when she was feeling this selfish. He released one arm, but the touch was immediately back as he put a finger beneath her chin and tipped it upward.

"There is nothing wrong with wanting more, Kelley. Don't think that there is. Wanting more saved my life."

She wanted to ask what that meant but her heart slammed in her chest. *Mack was more*. The kind of more she'd never wanted.

A tip of a finger teased her neck, and she closed her

eyes. Never was a long time. And right now she felt completely helpless to do anything but accept his light caress.

His chin dipped the slightest bit so that his lips were close to her temple.

Her chest rose and fell as sensations expanded inside her, shattering the reserve she'd clung to so tightly.

She held her breath, feeling yet again the rise of panic, but he stepped back. Looked at her for a long moment.

"God, you're beautiful."

"I'm not."

"Damned near the prettiest thing I've ever seen. You look like an angel."

"You're just saying that because of what I just said."

"No, I'm not. I'm telling you what I see. You're just trying to hide her. What I don't understand is why."

She really couldn't breathe now as his low voice seduced her. But the why was stuck in a big painful lump in her chest. It would always be there. He could never know the why.

"Stop hiding. For five minutes, stop hiding. I will if you will."

He came forward then, his body barring hers from walking away. Outside the storm howled, but the warmth of his body cocooned her, solid and warm. Mack raised his hand, grazed her jawline gently.

Everything in her went into a slow meltdown. This gentleness was so foreign, so sensual, she wasn't sure she could bear it. A tiny voice inside of her warned that he'd want more, but she pushed it away with a silent promise of *just this much*. She wanted to see, for once, if she could handle it.

His fingers traced the soft skin, over and over, touching her cheek. Their gazes locked for long moments as she contemplated what would happen next.

"This isn't a good idea," she whispered, hearing the longing in her own voice even as she denied him. And still the tips of his fingers stroked, a tactile kiss against skin. Taking his time.

"I know."

"I think you should go."

"I probably should."

"What do you want from me?" She trembled. She needed different words than she'd heard before. She wanted for once in her adult life to touch and be touched, kiss and be kissed without the mantle of fear cloaking her.

"A kiss," he murmured, his gaze following the path of his fingertips, the whole thing setting her body on fire. "I'd like one kiss."

His fingertips caressed, cupping her cheek as he took the last step in and claimed her mouth.

And oh, he was gentle. Her heart wept with the beauty of it as his soft lips touched hers, their breaths mingled in the silence as the candle flickered behind them. Touched again, then moved to graze the crests of her cheekbones, her closed eyes as she sighed. His right hand pulled her closer so that she fit lightly against his body, sensations heightened as much by the places they didn't touch as the ones where they did.

And still he kissed her, feather-light kisses on her

mouth until she finally raised her arms to his shoulders and kissed him back.

Mack closed his eyes against the onslaught of her taste as her fingers dug into his shoulder blades. His blood surged as her mouth opened beneath his, letting him in. He hadn't expected the sweetness, and he hadn't expected the heat. Both hit him like a fist in the gut. And with her small breasts pressed against his chest, he wanted more. One kiss wasn't enough, and the knowledge tore into him, leaving him questioning.

Tonight he'd wanted to kiss her, plain and simple. And not just because she deserved to feel beautiful and have someone mean it, not because she'd admitted she was afraid of the dark like he was, but because he wanted to.

Her body was warm against his and he opened his lips wider, demanding more. A sound growled up from his chest and into her mouth and he took a step forward, backing them against the solid counter.

Kelley felt his body press hers more firmly into the counter. The top dug into her and recalled her to her senses. Not this much. She had to stop it now. She had to keep control of the situation.

She wrenched her lips from his, sliding out from between his body and the Formica countertop.

"We need to stop," she breathed, skittering away to the main part of the room. Only once there she realized the only furniture was a bed and she felt the silent scream building. No. She would not lose control of the situation. Of herself.

He followed her.

"Kelley."

His tone was placating but she shook her head. "You've got to go. Now."

"It was just a kiss."

"No, it damn well wasn't," she replied, lifting her head and pinning him with her gaze. "I said no. I meant it."

The words gave her power she hadn't expected. There would be no negotiation. No backing down.

"Of course no means no. I just don't want to leave you like this. Upset. Please, talk to me."

She fought to keep her voice steady. "I need you to go. Dinner is over."

"All right, if that is what you truly want." He agreed but the syllables sounded frustrated and her heart continued to club away in her chest. He spun on his heel and went to the door, grabbing his jacket on the way.

"I'm next door if you need anything." He was gone with a gust of icy wind and the slam of the door. She rushed behind him and locked it with a click of the deadbolt, adding the chain for good measure.

Then she sat on the bed, touched her lips with shaking fingers. A laugh bubbled up from her belly, high pitched and disbelieving.

And when it faded away, the only other sound was that of her crying.

4

"**P**ulling out?"

Mack was watching her from the doorway of his motel room. At the sound of his voice she closed her eyes, exhaled, and pasted a smile on her face as she slammed the passenger door to the truck, wading through several inches of snow to the tailgate. She could handle this. She'd had lots of time to think while the snow had blown and drifted outside. In the end, she'd come to two conclusions. One, she still wanted to make Christmas dinner properly, and for that she needed his help. And two, she had to make it absolutely plain that their relationship was a working one. Cool. Distant. Professional.

"Gram's being released today."

"Oh, that's good news." His words made a warm curl around her insides that she found hard to ignore.

"Yes, it is." She tentatively met his eyes, unable to stop the relief sluicing through her at the good prognosis. "She's doing very well, her doctor says. I think we'll all feel better once she's back home where she belongs."

He leaned against the doorframe, one shoulder bolstering him up and looking like he hadn't a care in the world. His breath made clouds in the cool air and he'd shrugged on a jacket but left it unzipped.

"You made it through the storm okay, I see."

Small talk reduced them to redundancies. "Yes," she replied. The words came out softer than she intended as she remembered the long hours she'd sat awake, reliving things she didn't want to again, and finding them all mixed up with how good his kiss had felt. Too good. They'd simply gotten carried away. It was up to her to set things straight. To set the boundaries.

She ran her tongue over her bottom lip as if she could still taste him there. There could be no more kissing if she wanted to achieve her goal. It would only muddy the waters.

"About the dinner…" She leaned against the tailgate and put her hands into her coat pockets. "I want to hire you to teach me to cook Christmas dinner."

She put a slight emphasis on the word "hire." He had to understand.

"Hire me." His chin flattened. "I already said I'd help you. I don't need your money, Kelley."

"If anyone else hired you, they'd pay you for your time. I am no different.' She straightened her spine. This had to be about business only, and he needed to understand that. "Whatever your going rate is, that's fine."

"If this is about the other night…" His shoulder came away from the door frame.

"It's not," she shifted her purse in front of her. He should just stay where he was while she laid out the rules.

"Fair enough. You can hire me to teach you to cook."

She forced herself to lean against the tailgate of the truck. "Just let me know when I should come to the shop and I'll juggle some things around at home."

He considered for a moment. "It's going to be inconvenient for you, isn't it? Coming into Helena."

She shrugged, though he was right. Driving in and back while trying to keep Rocking H going and helping out with Gram was going to require some good time management skills. "I'll manage."

"You know, I haven't been out to Rocking H since I was a kid."

"You want to come to my house?" Her back stiffened. In her mind she'd rehearsed this conversation and it always had ended with her in a class at his shop. Not him, in her kitchen. Ever.

"I don't usually do house calls, but it's Christmas." His boyish smile was disarming. He continued on as if she hadn't painted a scowl on her face. "Why not? Save you a drive in. I go out to check on my house on the Ridge several times a week anyway, it's only a few minutes out of my way."

He made it sound almost like she was doing him the favor. It would make things infinitely easier for her. And Amelia was right next door. She raised one eyebrow. "Are you sure?"

He shifted his weight again, and she was glad he was in his stocking feet, his toes curled over the doorstep.

"You're in a special situation that's all. And you have enough on your plate. Merry Christmas." He sent her a wise-crack smile. "I'm normally a Scrooge. You should take advantage of my offer before it disappears."

Her hands fidgeted in the pockets of her coat as she remembered his kiss. It couldn't happen again. She'd thought she could handle it and she couldn't.

"Strictly cooking," she stated baldly, amazed at her own temerity. But they'd danced around it enough. If this were going to happen at her house, it had to be crystal clear.

"Scout's Honor." He grinned.

Her shoulders sagged with relief. "I don't know where to start…"

"Leave it to me. I'll come out tomorrow night after my six o'clock class finishes. We'll tackle your vegetable course."

She paused with her hand on the door handle of the old pickup. Good, safe, vegetables. She'd said what she had to, and he'd agreed.

"I live in what used to be the bunkhouse," she explained. "Are you sure this isn't too much of an imposition?"

"I'm sure," he replied. He pushed away from the frame, resting his hand on the edge of the door and looking pleased with himself. "Just be there."

❋

Kelley saw the headlights turn up the drive and stood, taking a nervous breath.

Yesterday she'd been oh-so aware of how she must appear to Mack. When he'd seen her at her truck, she'd been in her customary jeans and plaid shirt, bundled up in a sheepskin jacket. The uniform of a rancher. And it had served her well for a lot of years. She'd never wanted to draw attention to herself. Keeping herself competent and, well, sexless, had worked.

Right up to the point where Mack had kissed her. And had called her beautiful.

Maybe he'd meant it, probably he hadn't, but yesterday morning she'd had a sudden desire to look slightly more feminine than a cowpoke in the middle of a roundup. Which hardly made sense since her sole purpose had been to set boundaries.

The vehicle came to a stop outside her door and she brushed a hand down her sweater, picking an invisible piece of lint off it. She hadn't wanted to be too obvious, so she'd chosen her best jeans and a soft, thick-knit sweater in tan with a cowl collar. She'd put in earrings, tiny hoops rather than the plain gold studs she normally wore. She tightened her ponytail and took two complete breaths, trying to settle the nerves skittering around in her stomach.

He was here to show her to cook. It was certainly not a date. There nothing wrong with wanting to look decent rather than someone who'd just come in from the barn.

She met him on the porch, leaving the door open behind her. He got out of a sport utility and came around the back bumper. Her heart missed a beat, then caught its normal rhythm somewhat accelerated. Lord, he was handsome. The sheepskin collar of his leather jacket cradled his jaw, his breath formed clouds around his head. His dark hair and eyes stood out in the light from her doorway and he paused at the bottom of her steps, holding grocery bags in his hands.

The pause held for only a few seconds, but it was enough that Kelley felt vibrations humming between them. Maybe it hadn't been all in her head. All she knew for sure was that this was the first time in a long time that she was looking forward to being with a man. That in itself was an earth-shaking revelation. Once she'd laid out the rules, something had happened to her fear. It had gone into hiding. She'd actually been anticipating his arrival. Maybe because he'd backed off when she'd asked. Or that he'd agreed to her terms without reservation.

"You made it."

His smile lit up his face. "With time to spare."

She found herself returning the easy smile. "Well, you'd better come in. It's cold out."

Kelley stood back as he entered, the grocery bags dangling from his fingers. She reached out and took two, simply to give her hands something to do. It looked like he'd thought of everything, and she was momentarily intimidated. She was going to look stupid. She'd always considered herself modern, yet the fact that she couldn't cook was something else that made her feel distinctly unfeminine, whether it was wrong or right. It was just there.

No. She would do this. She just had to trust him to show her how.

"Kitchen's through there," she directed. It wasn't like he'd get lost. She felt her cheeks flush as she followed him. The house was small—a kitchen and living room downstairs, bathroom and bedroom in a loft upstairs. That was all. Four rooms, and a storeroom off the back. She realized how it must look to him. When she'd mentioned his name on the drive from the hospital, Gram had known all about the big fancy house he was building on the bluff. Kelley had kept her eyes on the road, surprised but simply happy Ruby had the energy to make idle chatter.

She started to see the small house through his eyes. She had the main house cast-off furniture from several years past, and very little in way of decoration. Amelia seemed to have inherited the decorating gene and when the family got together it was always at the main house.

"Kelley, are you coming or not?"

"Coming!"

She went into the kitchen. He had started unpacking bags and she reached out to help. "Did you bring the whole store?"She was shocked to see the mass of ingredients accumulating on her table.

"It's not as scary as it looks. It's like anything else. Get started, and finish when you're done. Come on...I'll show you how to peel a carrot."

Kelley was pleased he was taking her seriously and keeping things about work. They sat together at the table, companionably peeling potatoes, carrots, and chopping something Mack called pancetta.

"It looks like ham. Or bacon."

"It is. Kind of. It's not smoked, though. And we'll use the fat from cooking it to flavor the rest of the dish." He reached out to change how she held her knife and she held her breath. The last time he'd touched her this way she'd ended up in his arms. Her fingers shook and she relinquished the knife, took it back when he'd showed her. No more touching; it was too distracting.

"If you say so."

The potatoes, green beans and carrots were all put to boil while he showed her how to fry the pancetta, adding in sage and little bits of red pimiento. This time he didn't cradle her between his arms like he had with the phyllo; it was like by unspoken agreement they'd maintain their space. When the pancetta was done they removed it and cooked lemon, parsley and thyme in another pan. When everything was drained, Mack watched as she poured the lemon parsley mixture over the carrots, then put the beans to sauté lightly as she mashed the potatoes. With a growing sense of satisfaction, she measured out sour cream, cream cheese, butter and milk and added them to the smooth potatoes, added the pancetta mixture to the beans all under the tutelage of Mack's keen eye.

"Oh my word." Kelley looked around at her kitchen. Pots were everywhere. Potato and carrot peelings were still on the table. And she suddenly realized that despite the apparent success of the recipes, she had no serving dishes for anything.

"What's wrong?" He moved to her elbow. "You did wonderfully. Far better than I would have expected, considering the asparagus puffs disaster. We didn't even need a fire extinguisher."

She stared up at him, feeling slightly shell-shocked. "It's not that... I'm not ready for this. Look at my kitchen. If I make a mess like this in Amelia's kitchen, she'll..."

He pushed her into a chair and smiled indulgently. "First, you're going to breathe."

"I've finally bitten off more than I can chew."

"You haven't. You run a ranch nearly single handedly, in charge of how many men and head of cattle? Come on. A single dinner isn't going to be your downfall."

"Yes, but I know how to do that."

"Well, you weren't born knowing how to run a ranch. You know because you learned. Three days ago you were shredding phyllo. Tonight you've made lemon parsley carrots, green beans with pancetta and sage, and gorgeous mashed potatoes." His hand grazed her knee, leaving a trail of warmth. "You're just overwhelmed, that's all. Now that you're getting the hang of things, you'll be able to tidy as you go. Relax, and let me bring you a plate."

Kelley absently rubbed the spot he'd patted as he removed a pan from the oven and sliced an herb-crusted turkey breast he'd brought with him. When the plate was full, he brought it to her. "Taste that and believe."

Where he got his confidence in her, she had no idea. Tonight was a small battle in a big war in her opinion. She picked up her fork as Mack cleaned the table of their peelings. "Aren't you eating?"

"I'm making room. Go ahead, tell me what you think."

"I don't want to ruin it. It's so pretty." The potatoes were snowy white, contrasted with the vibrant orange and green of the other vegetables. The smell of the turkey breast had her stomach growling. She took her first bite of beans and her eyes widened. "It's good. I mean, really good!"

"Of course it is. And you did it. I just watched, and offered guidance."

He sat down with his own plate.

And the room got very quiet.

Kelley suddenly realized that for the second time in a week, they were sharing a meal.

"This feels weird."

"You'll get over it." He aimed another winning smile her way. How was it that he was so relaxed when she was completely tied up in knots, just from being near him?

The trouble was, Kelley *was* getting over it. She was starting to like him. Unlike the rough, domineering men she was used to, he didn't judge. Mack's patience and careful guidance gave her confidence. He hadn't questioned her rules and his easygoing manner had a way of inspiring her trust. If this was the true Mack, then she also knew he was very good at what he did. No wonder he'd made Mack's Kitchen such a success.

He'd done things that she'd only daydreamed about. She still resented it the tiniest bit, knowing he'd seen so much of the world while she'd been held here by an invisible leash. But it was hard to hate him for it when they were sitting in her kitchen, eating a meal he'd helped her cook. He didn't look like a millionaire. He looked like an ordinary guy in jeans and a sweater who just happened to be, perhaps, the best-looking man she'd ever known.

"Can I ask you a question?"

"Sure." He scooped up potatoes on his fork and took a bite. "You did a really good job with these, you know."

His praised warmed her. "Thank you."

"What's your question?"

She looked up, feeling suddenly shy. "You've traveled so much. I was just wondering…what's Paris like?"

"Paris?"

"I've…I've just never traveled."

He was quiet for a few moments, as if trying to decide.

"Paris is noisy, and hectic, and smelly. Of course, it's easy to love when it smells of the day's fresh bread, or when you're walking the Left Bank and you're assaulted with delicious scents from the restaurants and cafés. It rains like the devil and then the clouds open up and it's like beams of light from heaven." He grinned. "Of course, no trip is complete without Versailles. And you really realize why the revolution happened."

"Let them eat cake?"

His low laugh warmed her clear to her toes. "Precisely."

"And you've been to Italy? London?" She was hungry for the information now and leaned forward, encouraging him with a swoop of her fork.

He leaned back in his chair, toying with his glass of

water. "Of course. I spent a month eating my way through towns and markets in Tuscany. And London is just…London. I lived in Chelsea for a while. Sunday mornings we…I went walking in Battersea Park and drank cappuccino from a paper cup."

"It sounds wonderful."

"Christmas in London is like nowhere else." He smiled, but his eyes took a far away look and the curve of his lips faltered the smallest bit.

Did it hold some sadness about it for him? She wanted to ask, but it felt presumptuous. Besides, it went against the rules she'd set up. Cool. Distant. Professional.

Trouble was, the more they talked, the less distant she became.

"What's it like at Christmas, then?"

He sat back in his chair, his face taking on a faraway look. "There's skating at Somerset House, the lights in the West End. Then there's the Christmas tree in Trafalgar Square, and carolers…"

"Why did you come back?"

"Because this is home, Kelley." He met her eyes with quiet acceptance.

"But you have no one here."

The moment it was out of her mouth she wished she could take it back. Everyone in town knew that his mother had skipped off right after Mack had finished high school. Even though she'd barely known Mack, the story had caused a sensation in Rebel Ridge. His gaze slid away from hers and he picked up his glass of water.

What possessed her to point out he was alone…a week before the holiday?

She started to reach out but drew her hand back. She still wasn't comfortable touching him. "I'm sorry, Mack," she offered. "That was insensitive."

"It's okay. It's true."

She saw the line of his lips and the set of his jaw and knew she'd touched a nerve.

"How's your grandmother?"

She let him change the subject because clearly he was uncomfortable. The sudden realization he was going to be alone on Christmas settled in an empty place inside her. She had Gram, and Amelia and Jesse. But Mack had no one. For the briefest of moments, "Why don't you join us" hovered on her tongue. But she couldn't bring herself to say the words. Inviting someone for Christmas…well it was a family holiday. After the kiss they'd shared—she really didn't want it to be misconstrued. She wouldn't lead him on when nothing could come of it. And Lord only knew what Amelia and Gram would make of her inviting a man to Christmas dinner. So she kept the words inside and answered his question instead.

"She's doing well, but a bit slower. She tries not to show it, but when she thinks no one is looking…" Kelley wrinkled her brow. She couldn't help the worry. "She's not one to take it easy. I wish she'd be more patient. Let herself heal properly."

"If she's like I remember, she always went a mile a minute."

"Not now. And she's lost weight. She insists it's the

hospital food, but I know better. She's getting old, Mack. Nothing we can do to stop it, but it sure doesn't make it any easier. She raised us. And she's the only family we have left."

Mack leaned forward and put a warm hand on her knee beneath the table. "You obviously care for your family deeply. And they love you. I know she's ailing, but I envy you that, Kelley. I envy it very much."

All of her senses were focused on the warm spot his hand made on her leg. Normally she shied away from physical touches.

But normally there was no Mack. And he seemed to touch like it was the most natural thing in the world.

"You do? But you've done so much with your life."

"Yes, I have. And I never had to answer to anyone, either. There's something to be said for that."

"But?"

He smiled. "So you did sense the but."

Kelley wasn't sure if he realized it or not, but his thumb was drawing lazy circles on her leg. She should move it away, but it felt good. It didn't feel threatening. It felt right.

Finally his voice came low, and maybe with a trace of anger she hadn't heard before.

"Not everyone grows up that way. In my line of work, I see a lot of families that don't work. For whatever reason. People that are alone. Divorcees. Singles. Widowers. All searching for something. You came to me to help your family. You came to me to give something, not to find it. You're the exception, Kelley."

She didn't feel like the exception and didn't feel like

she was much of a giver, either. She was trying to hold things together, that was all. Trying to show she could do it, that there was more to her than what people saw at face value. But she couldn't go into all that with him.

"It's getting late," she murmured, trying hard to slow her heart rate. His hand was still touching her thigh. It was silly to let a simple touch affect her so much. She pushed away from the table and gathered the plates. "Thank you, Mack. Now I have an appetizer, and I can manage the vegetables. I think. Although I have no idea what to do with what's left over."

"I can take it for you if you want. If you have any plastic containers."

What on earth would he want her leftovers for? He was a cook, for goodness' sake! Surely he'd want to cook his own food, from fresh ingredients.

"I have a place I donate to regularly. Having a cooking school means sometimes there's surplus. If it means someone gets a decent meal, or any meal at all…"

Kelley looked up into his eyes. Mack Dennison was turning out to be a continual source of surprise. There was no putting on airs with him, despite the flashy SUV or the brand name clothing. "You're turning out to be a bit of a saint," she said lightly, while emotions within her churned.

"Hardly a saint," he murmured, taking advantage of her full hands and moving in to kiss her.

5

K elley's fingers tightened around the plates as Mack's lips on hers made everything in her body turn to jelly. It was the most delicious thing in the world. The perfect ending to a long day.

His fingers were firm on her upper arms and his body warm against hers. He took a step and she danced slowly backwards with him until her hips met with the countertop. Then there was no give between their bodies at all. His was firm and strong. And God help her, she liked it. That in itself was a revelation. It made her feel protected, not in danger.

The kiss broke off and his forehead rested against hers, his breath fanning her cheeks and doing nothing to relieve the unexpected vibrations humming through her body.

"I told myself I wasn't going to do that." His voice was ragged and rough, sexy enough to make her toes curl. "It's okay," she whispered, realizing that it indeed was. The air still crackled between them; the admission had done nothing to defuse the moment. If anything, she wanted him more. His apology told her he'd respected her boundaries. He'd backed off rather than pushing for more, and she was flattered that he'd wanted to kiss her again.

She turned to the side and deposited the dishes beside the sink. She had to take a step back. She wasn't prepared for him and was even less ready for the feelings that suddenly were cropping up. Anticipation. Desire. She didn't know what to do with that. She was used to being in charge, but that was work. Her personal life...well, she didn't exactly have a personal life, and it shocked her that for the first time in ages she actually wanted one. If she hadn't, then why had she made an effort to dress up tonight? And yet still deep down, fear tried to claw its way out, along with a certainty that she wasn't ready to take this relationship past friendship.

"I can't," she murmured, attempting to squirm out from between his body and the cupboards. She was fighting a ghost that shouldn't matter anymore and resented it. Mack made her want it to not matter at all.

She wished she could read his eyes as he watched her so closely, but she didn't have a clue what he was thinking. He must think her the most irritating woman. She knew she was blowing hot and cold. She'd get just so close, and then push away. She could still feel the heat of his hands on her skin and she swallowed.

She ached to be touched again but something held her back. There was a big gap between moving past *fear* and into *trust* territory; too large to leap across. "Could we just be friends, please? I'm not looking to get involved."

"As I recall, you were kissing me, too."

His dark eyes were unwavering. He put his hands in his jeans pockets, and she wanted to go wrap her arms around his ribs and snuggle in. Somehow he made her feel safe, and perhaps that was the most dangerous thing of all.

"I know." She could do this; she dealt with stubborn old ranch hands every day. She took a breath. "I need your help. I don't think I can pull a family Christmas off without it. But if we get involved…it will make a mess of things." She tried to think of it in terms he could relate to. "We're keeping the dishes I make simple, right? Let's just keep *us* the same way. If we make it too complicated…"

His dark eyes probed hers. "You're scared. Don't be. Kelley, friends can kiss. There are no rules against it. But we can take it slow if you want."

She would get through this, she would, and with some shred of dignity. Her hands were cold, and she rubbed the damp palms on her jeans. "We agreed to a professional relationship. I'd rather we stayed just… friends. I like having you as a friend, Mack."

MACK CLENCHED HIS FINGERS WITHIN THE DENIM pockets of his jeans, simply to keep from reaching out and touching her. He'd already broken his first rule— never get involved with a client. There'd been something about her in the motel room though, a soft vulnerability he found irresistible. She kissed him like she meant it, but then backed off. She had the other night, too, and he'd known he had to back away. Why was she afraid? And what was it about her that kept drawing him in, making him try again?

"The more I'm with you, the harder it is to be just your friend," he said honestly.

Her eyes widened further, but not with the desire he craved. Once again he saw the flash of fear. Why in the world would she be afraid of him? His hand slid out of his pocket and he took the steps necessary to reach her and take her hand. Wanting to reassure her. He lifted it to his cheek and pressed a small kiss to the back. Her hand was cold and questions popped into his head. "I know something's going on with you. But...everyone has wounds, Kelley."

KELLEY FLINCHED, BUT DIDN'T BREAK EYE CONTACT. Pain, humiliation, self-loathing, disgust...she remembered those feelings well enough and they had crippled her for years. Now, when she really wanted to move past them, it made her angry that they still held her back.

And she sure as hell couldn't tell him why.

"Even you?" She let him keep her fingers within his, the contact was strangely soothing.

"Even me."

He hesitated, and she got the sense he was picking and choosing what to tell and what not to. She'd done it often enough herself. Measuring words, avoiding eye contact until a decision had been made. She knew he'd chosen his words when he looked fully into her face.

"Let's just say, not everyone has an ideal upbringing. And things happen that color their lives. Things happen that you cannot change or take back."

His words struck a painful chord with her. But she knew he wouldn't understand this. Even after a decade, she found it impossible to understand. "It doesn't matter."

He sighed. "If you ever want to talk about it, let me know. I'm here."

His dark eyes felt like they could see clear through her and accepted her for who she was. That in itself was a novelty. Somehow they'd ended up not only kissing, but more importantly, talking.

He stacked the last container of leftovers, preparing to leave. "I just want you to know that I think what you're trying to do for your family is a good thing."

She shook her head. "This is no big sacrifice on my part. I love them."

"You're the glue holding the family together, Kelley. If I can see it, I hope they can too."

Kelley blinked at the unsolicited praise. It was inconceivable that she was the glue. She was just Kelley who ran the ranch.

He was going to be alone at Christmas. It ceased to matter what Amelia or Gram would say. She would explain. They would understand—no one should spend the holidays alone.

She leaned forward, holding out one hand in invitation. "Why don't you come to Christmas dinner?"

He balanced the containers while shock glimmered on his face. "You're inviting me to your family dinner?"

"Do you have somewhere else you need to be?"

He didn't answer right away, and she suddenly realized maybe she'd been presumptuous. Maybe he did have someplace special to go.

"I'm not a charity case, Kelley. I don't want you to ask me because I told you I was alone. I'm fine. The last thing I want is for you to feel obligated."

She smiled. Pride she understood. "Heck, I'm not obligated. I'm paying you for your time. This is off the clock and offered in friendship, Mack. Nothing more. Come to dinner with friends."

He blinked twice. "I'd be honored to come."

"Honored?" It was an unexpected compliment. No one ever seemed *honored* when she did something. She was struck again by the gentleness in his voice.

"Maybe it beats sitting in a motel room by myself watching 'It's a Wonderful Life.'"

He tried to make light, but she could see through it. "Will you see your mom over the holidays?"

"You know my mom left Rebel Ridge several years ago." His lips were set in a way that let her know the subject was closed. "I'm spending Christmas Eve at the shelter, serving dinner. And Christmas afternoon..." he paused, his eyes skittering away from hers for a moment, "at a rehab center in Helena."

He had no one, and spent his holiday with others who had no one, too. The absolute loneliness struck Kelley square in the chest. As long as she could remember, they'd had presents and a special family breakfast, winding up with a traditional Christmas dinner. Stockings were hung and old Bing Crosby carols played. The very thought of someone spending the holiday without any of that was impossible.

"Then I'm very glad you're joining us."

He cleared his throat. "Me, too."

WORDLESSLY HE GATHERED UP HIS LEFTOVERS AND WENT to the door. She followed him and held it open as he shrugged into his jacket. They'd just come to an agreement, so why on earth was he feeling like everything was suddenly more out of control?

At the bottom of the steps he turned to find her standing in the doorway again, the glow from the porch light shining off her hair. With her soft smile, she reminded him of an angel. His heart skipped as she raised a hand in farewell.

He lifted his own and went to his truck, his breath forming clouds in the chilly air. Maybe he should have told her the whole truth. But they'd forged a friendship tonight, and the last thing he wanted to do is endanger it. In the long run, it wouldn't make any difference.

He started the truck and looked back at the house. She was gone inside out of the cold and the door was shut. As he put the truck in reverse, he wished for the first time in a long time that it wouldn't make any difference at all.

"Easy. Shhh." Kelley held Risky's halter while Mack stayed outside the stall, quietly watching. "I'm sorry, Dr. Laramie. He's usually not this jumpy." Dr. Cooper, the regular vet, was on holidays. Andrew Laramie was his locum, filling in. Risky could sense a stranger despite Laramie's patient and soothing voice.

It had been three days since the kissing incident in her kitchen. Today Mack had brought the turkey as promised. They had worked companionably, preparing the turkey and stuffing and putting it in the oven. They'd bantered and teased. As friends. And yet…she wished he'd look at her *that* way again.

He was in her thoughts all the time. As she took care of stock, checked fences, supervised the hands, he was there on the fringes of her mind, with his casual touches, ready smile, soft seductive kisses. She didn't want to, and hadn't seen it coming, but she was falling for him.

But all of that had fled her mind with Risky's emergency. She'd had her hands full of soapy water when one of the hands had arrived at the door saying Risky'd been cut. She'd dropped everything in the kitchen and rushed to the barn, Mack right on her heels. She'd had the big bay gelding since she was fifteen. And when she saw the blood seeping from the gash, she knew stitches were the best plan.

Dr. Laramie gritted his teeth. "I'd rather not sedate unless it's necessary. But I think he should be stitched, and for that I'm going to have to."

Risky tossed his head once more. "Risky. Hush now."

Her muscles ached from keeping a firm hold on the

halter. Even though Risky was cross-tied, his agitation meant Laramie couldn't put in the sutures. For a moment she considered letting the wound go, letting it heal on its own. She met the vet's eyes and asked the question silently.

"It's up to you. It's deep enough to stitch but you could get away with it. Just."

Kelley turned away. Mack was watching her steadily, yet with a vigilance that made her feel like he'd be there if she needed him. He didn't step in, didn't offer an opinion. His implied confidence in her was a rarity. Most often the men she knew would either be telling her what they would do or disregarding her altogether. That Mack didn't, said as much about him as it did about her.

She looked back at Risky and gave his neck a reassuring rub. She hated sedation. There was something about making a creature so vulnerable that she resisted.

"No, you're right. If you're going to stitch it, he needs sedation." A vicious jerk left her shoulder aching. As the vet prepared the needles required, she tried to calm Risky. But his eyes were wild and she knew he was afraid and everything she did seemed to make it worse.

"He knows you're scared for him." Mack's voice was soft in her ear, but sure. His warm breath sent tingles down her body. "Let me try."

She stood back, relinquishing her hold on the halter. She could use the few moments to rest her arms. "Let me know when you've had enough. He's strong."

He didn't touch the halter at all but held out his hand, palm up. Risky sniffed, nudged. Mack stepped in and stroked the horse's jaw. And Kelley heard him

muttering words, words she couldn't make out, but
Risky stopped jumping and skittering through the stall.
The whites of his eyes disappeared, and the anxious
stamping of hooves gentled. Dr. Laramie waited only a
few moments. Standing perfectly still, eyes fastened on
Mack, Risky received the medication with merely a
twitch of his hide.

MACK PLACED HIS HANDS ON RISKY'S HEAD AND RUBBED
softly, uttering soft words while he blinked rapidly. He
hadn't expected such a complete reaction…not within
the horse and definitely not within himself. He'd merely
wanted to try—he'd seen Kelley's wince of pain as she
struggled to hold the horse's head.

She had more on her plate than he'd initially realized, and he also knew there was something holding her
back. She'd been so jumpy after a few simple kisses. He
wanted her to trust him with more than a dinner. And
the simple truth was that the gelding was afraid and in
pain. It reminded Mack of the many times he'd been
the same way. And how much work it had been to pull
himself out. If Risky could trust him, then perhaps
Kelley would, too.

"Mack…"

"Shhh," he uttered, ignoring Kelley, softly stroking
Risky's muzzle as the drugs took hold. For a moment he
felt an undeniable sadness that the animal had to be
sedated. Turned into a ghost of itself, numb against the
pain. Mack had lived that way far too long, without
benefit of drugs or alcohol. And as he finally met

Kelley's eyes across the stall, he knew it was time to start living again.

"How did you do that?"

The glow of approval on her face made him feel ten feet tall. He looked at Risky and murmured, "He just needed someone to talk to." He paused. "How's the vet doing?"

"I'm halfway there, thanks," came the voice from deeper in the stall. "Won't be long now."

Still Mack stroked softly, murmuring reassurances to the animal as Laramie put in the sutures.

When the stitching was done, Kelley watched as Mack relinquished his hold on Risky and stepped out of the stall, back into the corner once again. She listened with only half an ear as Laramie gave her instructions for caring for the wound…it was all things she knew already. What she really wanted to know was how did Mack know how to calm a frantic horse? And why was she just seeing this side of him now?

Watching him talk to Risky had sent a wave of love over her she could scarcely comprehend. In that moment he'd been different. He'd been tall and strong and capable and a man that she felt she could somehow lean on. He was just Mack. He'd dominated Risky with kindness and not force. Would he be that gentle with her? Her eyes had fixated on his hands, softly stroking, soothing. Would his hands be equally as tender on her skin? It was a revelation to her that she even desired it. That she was considering taking that leap, after so many years celibate and with a man she'd truly known such a short time. Time had ceased to matter, because in her heart she felt she could trust him. She didn't want to be just friends. Up until this moment, it had seemed the only option. But maybe, just maybe, Mack had changed all of that.

She blinked, took a step back, collecting scraps of bandage for the garbage. And then what? Where could they possibly go, together? She thought about her sister and how she'd rushed into a relationship, had her heart broken by Jesse's father, and how difficult it had been being a single mother. She thought of her own history and the weight it would bring to a new relationship. She was being fanciful. And there was no time for that.

Dr. Laramie was shaking Mack's hand when she turned back around.

"Thanks for your help."

"No problem." Mack looked more at home in the barn than Kelley could have imagined. With his jeans and heavy jacket, he could have been one of the hands helping out.

"Just a question," the vet asked. How did you learn to do that? He responded very well to you."

Mack laughed. "I used to work at a farm outside Rebel Ridge. I always had a soft spot for the horses. Why?"Laramie bent to grab his case. "I'm only filling in for Cooper while he has Christmas with his family. After that…well, I'm going home myself. A ranch in Alberta," he continued. "It's going to take a few months to get the details straightened out, but I'm setting up a rescue operation. I spent a lot of time working with thorough-breds, and it's really hard watching them be put down when their run is done. Or seeing an animal that's been abused. I had enough and quit. We could use a few guys like you. You have a real way."

"Thoroughbreds...wait, Andrew Laramie. You worked with racehorses, didn't you?"

Laramie nodded. "That's right."

"I remember you...I think it was the Breeder's Cup last year. I was there watching with several of our investors."

It was a reminder that Mack lived in a world different from the Rocking H. Different from hers. Kelley aimed a bright smile at Laramie. "Mack is more than a ranch hand."She made the declaration with a certain sense of pride. She wouldn't have done that a few weeks ago. She *was* proud of him, she discovered. He was good at what he did, and successful. It couldn't have been easy, not when he started from nothing, no matter what he said. "He owns the Mack's Kitchen franchises."

Andrew grinned. "I know someone who'd love to do what you do, Mack. Personally, I don't know the right end of a spatula."

"Our newest location is opening up in Washington in January. I'm heading up there for the launch. We're always looking for franchise opportunities."

Kelley looked at her feet as the three of them walked down the corridor to the doors. He really would be leaving, then. After such a short time, she was getting used to having him around. Mack's arm brushed hers as Laramie laughed lightly.

"Might be difficult. *She* lives north of the border. Owns the bakery in Larch Valley and makes the best brownies I ever tasted." His mouth twisted. "Then there's the tiny problem that she won't speak to me."

Mack's fingers found hers and squeezed. She couldn't look at him. If she did, he'd know how much a simple handclasp affected her. It made her feel part of a couple, and that was a novelty. She'd been on her own so long it was a revelation to be a part of a united front. In the back of her mind she knew he would be going back to his life after Christmas. In her heart, at this moment, it didn't matter.

"Well, good luck with that," Mack offered. "Setting up a ranch can't be anywhere near as hard as thawing a woman's heart."

Laramie sent him a significant look. "Amen, brother."

She bit her lip. Did Mack think she needed thawing? She knew it was true. She knew she'd closed herself off for too long. What he didn't know is that he'd already thawed the ice around her heart. Could she show him that and still leave her heart intact when he was gone?

Laramie raised a hand in a wave and strode off to his truck, while Mack and Kelley stood in the frosty air outside the barn.

Kelley sighed, looking up at the crystal-blue sky—a sharp contrast to the pristine snow. Seeing Mack here, comfortable in her world, only made the attraction to him stronger. Was it so wrong to want to grab on to any bit of happiness, even if it was only for now?

"Kel?"

She turned to look up at him, saw his dark eyes twinkling back, saw a hint of stubble on his jaw that made her want to run her fingertips along the roughness.

"Hmmm?"

"Has it occurred to you that we left a turkey in the oven?"

"Oh no!"

Together they sprinted through the snow to the house, and Kelley flung open the door. There was no smoke, but an acrid odour wafted in from the kitchen and she ran forward with a cry.

"Wait!" Mac commanded. He bustled through, opening the back door and windows first. "Let me."

He reached into the oven as thin tendrils of smoke came out. Kelley pressed her fingers to her lips as she tried not to laugh at the sight. It wasn't all funny...she had a dinner in a few days and the trial run for the main event was a disaster. But the look on Mack's face... A giggle escaped.

He put the roaster on the stove top and stared at it. Kelley found him as sexy in a pair of oven mitts as she had when he'd held Risky's halter. Maybe more so.

"If my partners saw this..." He shook his head. "They'd be backing out in a hurry."

"Andrew Laramie would give you a job."

He angled a wry look in her direction. "Ha, ha."

Kelley stepped ahead, picked up a fork, and poked at the bird. "Yep. Definitely done."

"You're not upset."

She smiled. "Oh Mack, this is one time I couldn't care less."

"But I thought..."

And as the words hung in the air, something clicked into place. For the first time, she was completely comfortable with a man. She trusted him. The dinner didn't matter. Nothing mattered, except feeling free for the first time. He had done that. Just by being him.

In this moment, the past ceased to exist, and as it melted away so did the terror, the uncertainty, all of it. He had been careful with her from the start. She'd seen his hands, his wide, big hands so gentle on Risky's halter today, his voice soft and soothing. He was a man who understood pain and hurt and regret and she knew without a doubt that she could trust him.

The Christmas CD they'd put in the stereo was still playing, over and over and it no longer mattered what might happen in the future. She didn't care that they were from different worlds. He was here now. It was Christmas. If ever there was a time to take a chance, it was in this moment.

In the space of a heartbeat, she pressed her body against his, her lips on his lips.

She opened her mouth, meeting him equally. For once she felt blessed to be tall as their curves fit together like nesting eggs, his frame only a few inches ahead of hers. His kiss was like all the best things of Christmas… candlelight and gingerbread and the excitement of waking at four in the morning to open presents. She smiled against his mouth and found the hem of his sweater, snuck her hands underneath it and spread them wide over the heated skin of his back, marveling at the smooth strength of it.

He broke off the kiss, breathing heavily. "You said you wanted…"

"I changed my mind."

"Why?"

She leaned back far enough so she could see his face. He meant it. He really meant it. He wasn't pushing but asking permission in his own way. Her heart soared with the realization.

"Because I want you, all of you." The words came out, filled the room, filled her heart because she meant them.

"You want me."

The indecision in his voice tore at her heart. Had no one ever wanted him before? It was inconceivable. His dark eyes clung to hers, tacitly asking—he was a man who would always ask, never take.

Never before had she felt sexually powerful, but she did now. She ran her tongue over her bottom lip, suddenly so sure that it almost made her laugh with the joy of it. The freedom was energizing. "I want you. I want all of you."

If she thought he'd hesitate further, she was wrong. His hand, his very capable hand, the one that had calmed her horse and made delicate pastry in a dingy motel room now cupped her neck firmly as he dragged her close again. His fingers deftly slid her buttons through the buttonholes, and she held her breath as he pushed the shirt off her shoulders. But none of the gut-knotting fear came. Only intense pleasure and anticipation.

His sweater joined her shirt on the floor and their

skin was pressed together, hot and firm and oh-so wonderful without the barrier of fabric between them. She took his hand and led him upstairs to the loft, shaking a little as she realized what she was asking. She was asking him to make love to her, and it was exhilarating and terrifying all at once.

"Do you have protection?"

"You don't?"

He couldn't possibly know how silly that question was. Of course she didn't have anything resembling birth control; there'd never been any need. But rather than say it and ruin what progress they'd made, she answered simply. "No, I don't." And hoped he did.

He slid his wallet from his jeans and withdrew a foil packet. "I have one."

"For emergencies?" She raised an eyebrow, surprised at her own temerity.

His responding grin was dangerously sexy. "Exactly."

She lifted her chin, suddenly realizing she was standing before him in her underwear and that his hungry eyes were taking in every inch of bare skin. She pushed away the shyness threatening to take over and smiled softly. "And this is an emergency?"

Dark eyes glittered at her. "Oh honey, you've no idea."

He took a step forward, but she stopped him once more. In one way she was teasing, but in another found she wanted to know. "How long has that been in there?"

And as he reached for her, he growled, "Long enough."

6

Mack closed his eyes, savoring the feeling and the taste of her that lingered in his mouth. Right now, Kelley's head rested on his chest, the blond hair falling over her face while her arm was looped around his midsection. She was sleeping; he could tell by the slow, hot breaths that dampened his chest.

Lord, she'd been sweet. And fairly innocent, he was sure. It was in the way she touched, with a hint of shy hesitancy, like she wanted him to take the lead. It had been fresh, like a spring rain. The women he knew weren't like that. But Kelley…

He sighed and closed his eyes, feeling her warmth curled around him. He hadn't wanted to care about a woman for a very long time. Not since Christmas two years ago. That was when everything had changed. Oh, he'd believed in love once. But it had been a hard lesson to learn.

Her arm tightened around his ribs and he held his

breath, not wanting to disturb her. He'd let things go this far and he shouldn't have. Now he'd gone and spent the night—another rule broken. He rubbed a hand over the stubble on his face. And yet he couldn't find it within himself to regret it. That in itself sent off alarm bells in his head. It was well and good for her to need his help. It wasn't good when he started feeling attached.

"Mack?" She said his name in a husky whisper that reached right to the middle of him and grabbed.

"What, Kelley?"

And damned if she didn't laugh, a low, sexy rumble that came right from her toes and out her heart.

"That was good, Mack."

He smiled, lifted his head, and kissed her hair, determined not to ruin the morning. "I know."

"No, I mean really good. Better than I expected."

He couldn't stop the smile that spread on to his face. "You gotta stop setting your expectations so low…"

She laughed, a sexy little p.s. that did funny things to his insides. "I'm glad you stayed."

Suddenly he was, too. Even if it did complicate things more than he was strictly comfortable with.

"Do you want coffee?"

"Mmmm. You making it?"

"Sure."

She snuggled into him and he felt other parts of his body wake up. He had to move now, or they'd never get out of bed. And he didn't think a repeat of last night was the best of plans.

"I'll be back in a few minutes."

When he came back, mugs in hand, she'd fallen

asleep again, her hair and the sheets a sexy tangle. He wet his lips, wondering what the hell he'd been thinking. It wasn't the sex. It was Kelley, and the fact that he cared about her—too much. Right now he wanted to gather her up in his arms and hold her close—every soft, sweet-scented inch of her.

That hadn't been part of the plan. He should have known better than to spend the night. He cleared his throat. "Your coffee, madam."

KELLEY DRAGGED HERSELF OUT OF SLEEP, PROPELLED BY the amazing smell. She blinked, opened her eyes, and saw Mack sitting on the edge of the bed, smiling and holding out a mug of steaming brew.

"Good morning." She moved to sit up and froze.

She was naked! And here was Mack in his jeans and shirt, partly unbuttoned so she could see a generous slice of the hard chest beneath it. She dimly remembered waking a while ago, snuggling into his body…her face flamed. In the bright light of morning, the magnitude of what they'd done hit her with full force. She'd had sex. With Mack Dennison. She put her hands to her red face and Mack laughed.

"That's charming," he said. He still held the coffee out and she wanted it…badly. She could hide her blushing face behind the mug. How was a woman supposed to act the morning after? She had no idea. Her sum total experience had been limping home from prom and hiding her soiled dress in the back of the closet until she could burn it.

Holding the quilt to her chest, she wiggled until she was sitting in the bed, and reached for the mug.

She took a hot sip and closed her eyes. Delicious. When she opened them, Mack leaned over and kissed her gently. Chaste, if it came down to it. If it could be chaste considering what had passed between them last night.

"I'll make us some breakfast." Mack reached for his coffee that he'd put on the dresser. She tried not to be disappointed that he didn't crawl under the covers with her.

"I'm awfully glad you're here." Her heart blossomed as she realized how true it was. "And I'm so pleased you're spending Christmas with us. Amelia always gets the most beautiful tree. And her pecan pie...you haven't lived until you've had her pie."

A shadow passed over his face and Kelley frowned. What had she said that was wrong? She sensed defiance in the set of his jaw, but more than that. Hurt. Her heart melted just a little bit knowing it.

She held the covers to her chest with her arms and put her free hand on his wrist, feeling the pulse there thrum beneath her fingers. "What is it? What did I say?"

He raised his head and she stared into his eyes. She could so easily get lost in the chocolatey depths of them.

He turned his hand over and twined his fingers with hers. "When you talk about Christmas..."

Her breath held. Was he going to back out? Was it too much too soon? She hadn't planned any of this. And she was pretty sure he hadn't, either.

"I don't really talk about this, but when you speak of

the holidays and traditions and that sort of thing…well, you should know I've never had a real Christmas."

"Never?"

"Never."

"No tree, turkey, and presents?"

He laughed, a bitter, jerky sound. "Not ever. Not even close. My holidays normally consist of tasteful trees in a hotel lobby and a dinner in a five-star restaurant."

She couldn't imagine December twenty-fifth coming and going without a proper celebration. Her heart ached for the childhood magic he must have missed. "That's the loneliest thing I've ever heard. I don't understand."

MACK KNEW IT WAS BETTER SHE KNEW THE TRUTH NOW. He had no illusions into the so-called magic of the season, didn't go in for the sappy sentimentality of peace on earth and goodwill towards men. In his house, there'd never been Santa Claus, or dinners, or any magic of any sort. Why start now, only for himself?

There'd always been a little voice in the back of his mind saying he hadn't deserved it. In his head, he knew that was a lie. But in his heart, where it mattered, he'd never been able to shake the thought completely.

He'd tried once and had failed utterly. He knew there was always a crash at the end of the buildup. It was better she knew the truth now. He wasn't who she thought he was.

"There was never money for Christmas—or much desire to put in the effort, either. Not when the priority was making sure there was enough vodka in the house to get through the season. That's what happens when you grow up with an alcoholic."

"Your mother?"

He heard the gasp that accompanied the explanation and hated it. "That's right," he confirmed. He hooked his thumbs in the tabs of his pockets. "A drunk who cared more about her next bottle than feeding her kid."

"I never guessed…"

She met his gaze; he challenged her with his eyes. "No one did."

"Oh, Mack, how awful for you." Her eyes softened and he tried very hard to hate her for pitying him. "So you really never had Christmas when you were a boy?"

He looked away, determined not to feel like the little lost boy any longer. He'd grown up. Made a success of himself. "She tried a few times. It just never quite worked out in a 'White Christmas' sort of way, you know? And now…there doesn't seem to be a point. It's just me, and with the business, it's our busiest retail season. The closest I get is decking out the stores and bringing in seasonal stock."

"I'm sorry, Mack. About your mom. About all of it."

He hadn't wanted to delve further into his past, but he'd rather she walked away now before either of them got in too deep. "I took home ec so I could learn to feed myself. By the time I was a teenager, I had a teenager's appetite. And boxed mac and cheese can only fill a kid's stomach for so long."

"Oh Mack." She sighed his name, lifted their joined hands and placed a kiss on the back of his thumb.

He shifted on the covers, pulling his hand out of her grasp. "You see? That's why I didn't tell you before. Now you pity me. And I don't want your pity. I never wanted anyone's pity."

"Can't I feel sorry for the boy?"

His anger flared. "No. That boy doesn't exist anymore. I discovered I liked cooking. I was good at it. I got a job at a farm after school and on weekends and used my wages to put food on my own table. Later I used the money to study. And I got backing to open my first Mack's Kitchen."

"Then why so angry? Why so secretive? No one would think any less of you…"

He's teeth clenched almost painfully as he heard sympathy in her voice. "Don't you?" he bit out. "Don't you see me differently now?"

"Yes. I see you as a kid who overcame a lot of odds to make himself a success." She readjusted the sheet and leaned close to him, forcing him to look at her. "There's no shame in that, Mack. It's admirable."

"I don't want the past to define me. I want the present. The future."

"And it does. Look at how successful you've become."

"Stop, please."

"Did you think people would think less of you if they knew? That I would?"

That's exactly what he'd thought. Plus he'd started having to deal with publicity with the success of the stores. The last thing he wanted was to capitalize on his childhood woes. Some things should remain private.

"I didn't want those days to be used to sell a product. I refuse to let my life be a rag-to-riches sob story."

Kelley smiled softly. She wasn't patronizing him or indulging him in any way. She looked so calm, so beautiful. Like she understood. But how could that be? "You just want to get on with it, do it on your own. You don't want to need anyone. Oh Mack, we're more alike than you might think."

She leaned up and kissed his cheek. "Thank you for trusting me," she whispered. He was surprised to see her eyes mist over, but then she blinked, and he wondered if he'd imagined it. He'd meant to tell her as a warning, that was all. A taste of what she was getting herself into. Giving her the opportunity to back away now. Instead she turned the tables on him and was pleased he'd trusted her, when trust had little to do with it.

He was getting in deeper by the second.

"It occurs to me that we're both abysmal at holiday traditions." She sat up on her knees and reached for her bathrobe. "So here's what we're going to do. This place is completely devoid of holiday spirit. We're going to get a Christmas tree. Then we're going to go shopping and get decorations."

"Shopping?" He didn't attempt to hide the cynicism in his voice, but she continued undaunted.

"I don't even have a wreath or sprig of mistletoe." She dropped a peck on his lips and they fell open, amazed at this new, bubbly, tactile Kelley.

"The mall opens at noon," she chirped, tying the

robe belt around her waist. "That leaves us this morning to find the perfect tree."

He raised his eyebrows. Silence hummed for a few seconds. This wasn't what he'd intended when he'd told her about his past. With one finger he reached over and tipped up her chin. "Maybe I want to spend the day with you. Just you. It's not often I get a day off this time of year, you know."

An adorable blush colored her cheeks. "So spend the day with me. We'll spend ridiculous amounts of money on Christmas kitsch. It'll be new."

She leaned over and kissed him, long and soft and sweet. "I want to do this for you, Mack. For both of us."

He couldn't resist her when she kissed him that way, full of promise and sweetness. He'd do it, but only for her. If she still believed a fairy-tale Christmas existed, he wouldn't be the one to play Scrooge.

"As long as you don't make me sing along with carols on the radio, fine. And when we come back, I'll make you the best hot cocoa you've ever tasted." He ran a finger down the column of her throat. "Of course, it does mean you'll have to get dressed, and that's a bit of a shame."

"If we're going searching for a tree, we'd better get started." She blinked innocently.

"You," he said, pointing a finger and getting up off the bed, "Are the devil to resist when you act like an angel." He kissed her forehead and then stopped at the bedroom door looking back over his shoulder. "How do you like your eggs?"

Her answer prompted a peal of laughter from him that lasted all the way down the stairs.

MACK TUGGED THE TOBOGGAN BEHIND HIM, MAKING tracks that Kelley stepped in, following him to the edge of the pasture and the tree line. The cloud ceiling was high, and snowflakes fell around them, cocooning them in a shushing sound. For a few precious minutes, it was as if they were the only two people in the world. The flakes floated to the ground, laying gently on the white blanket already there from the previous blizzard. He paused for a moment, and Kelley came up beside him, the clouds of their breaths mingling in the cold air. Fat snowflakes landed on her hat, while her hazel eyes appeared even more green against the flush of her cheeks. He inhaled, his chest expanding, while the valley lay below them, Christmas-card perfect.

He was tugging a toboggan and carrying an axe to cut down a Christmas tree. It was inconceivable. He turned from the scene and began pulling again.

There had been an awkward moment when they'd gone to the main house to ask to borrow Jesse's sled to haul the tree back with. He'd said hello to Mrs. Hughes —who'd acted like nothing was out of the ordinary and insisted he call her Ruby. But Amelia had given him a speculative look he wasn't sure he'd liked. He'd felt under a microscope, as he had many times as a boy. Like he was being measured and found wanting.

"So who was this Boone guy anyway?" Mack called back to Kelley, who was clumping along in her boots.

"Some guy that rescued Amelia and Jesse during the blizzard and stayed on to work. But he's gone now."

"You didn't like him."

When the footsteps stopped behind him, he paused and looked over his shoulder. Kelley had stopped, her hands on her hips.

"I didn't trust him. That's all. He wasn't exactly truthful about his reasons for being here. He pretended to be the hand I'd hired on. And Amelia hasn't always shown the best judgment."

He bit his tongue. Guilt trickled through him. He hadn't been completely truthful with Kelley this morning, either. But he'd already revealed more than he had planned on telling a woman ever again.

Kelley had stopped, put her mittened hands into the pockets of a grey wool coat. A pink knitted hat covered her ears, but her blonde curls cascaded over her shoulders. She looked like a winter angel.

"Maybe you should trust her more. We all made mistakes when we were younger."

"I'm just looking out for her. I'm her big sister. Jesse's father hurt her deeply. Am I wrong for not wanting that to happen again?"

"She's a big girl, Kelley. Old enough to know what she wants. Old enough to live with her own mistakes."

Kelley scowled. "That's what she said."

He laughed, turned around and started pulling again. "So what would she say if she knew about you and me last night?"

He kept his back to her, kept pulling even though he'd liked to have seen her face. After several more steps in silence, she answered.

"She does know. You were parked in my driveway all night. And she said be careful."

He stopped, dropping the cord to the toboggan and turned. She was only a step and a half away, her eyes gleaming in the brightness of reflected snow. There was a relief in not sneaking around.

"And are you? Careful?"

"It sure doesn't feel that way."

He took the extra step and put his gloved hands on her arms. "Then don't be careful for a little while longer, okay?" He wanted her this free, this unexpected, for a bit longer. Guileless and open. The holiday would be over soon, and he didn't want to ruin it for her. Christmas day was a day to be borne, that was all. Kelley was a balm against all of it.

He dipped his head and kissed her. She was soft and sweet and even innocent, despite what had transpired between them last night. "We can talk about her later," he murmured, his lips close to her cheek. "Right now, I've found you the perfect tree."

He stepped to the toboggan. He picked up the ax and made a well-aimed cut at the trunk of a fully rounded evergreen.

Kelley stood back and watched as Mack took swing after swing with the ax. A short week ago if someone had told her she'd be cutting a Christmas tree with Mack Dennison after a night of lovemaking, she would have laughed in their face. If they'd told her she'd be tromping through the snow in a borrowed coat and wearing pink—a color she tended to avoid in her line of work—she would have called them crazy. But here she was. She hadn't thought of him in terms of a lover. *Her lover.* And now whenever he was around, she felt the urge to girlify herself. For the first time ever, she felt as if she didn't have to hide her feminine side…and she liked it.

She wanted Mack for more than Christmas, and yet she wasn't sure how it could work. There'd been a brief idea that Boone would be staying on and it would have been welcome help to Kelley, despite her reservations about his relationship with Amelia. But now…he was gone. She was tied to Rocking H. And Mack was definitely tied to his business. She had to be realistic. She kept the thought around her like armor, even as she watched him, legs spread wide, shoulders flexing as he chopped down a perfectly shaped spruce tree. His breath made clouds as he struck the tree and exhaled. With a crack, the trunk gave and toppled over, a white cloud erupting in the snow as the branches splayed out.

She'd started out wanting to make Christmas for the family. Now that included Mack, too. What he'd told her this morning had been such a complete surprise. It was high time he had someone do something for him. It was unfamiliar territory, but one she thought they could enjoy discovering together.

Together they loaded the tree onto the sled and began the journey back to the house. Once back, Mack propped the tree up on the verandah and dusted off his hands. "Where's the stand?"

Kelley pulled off her mittens. "I don't have one."

"You don't?"

She smiled a little. "Don't act so surprised. We always celebrate at the main house. I guess we'll just have to get one in town today. Amelia already has a tree set up. She put it up for Jesse days ago."

"He's a cute kid."

Kelley grinned. "He is, isn't he? He made a wish for a daddy this year."

Mack had a strange look on his face, a mix of pity and pain and withdrawal. Kelley wrinkled her brow. After what he'd told her this morning, she should have thought before opening her mouth.

"I didn't think…" she rushed to apologize.

He put his arm around her waist and gave a squeeze. "It's alright. I feel for the kid though. Feeling like you're different is a hard thing to get used to. You look for ways to fit in. To hide it."

"Or you bury your nose in a book."

"Voice of experience?"

There was something in his voice that was almost defensive and she wondered at the strange turn of conversation. "No more than yours. You must have found it so difficult."

"Kelley…"

She raised a hand. "I know. You don't want pity. You don't want to talk about it."

"No, I don't."

It wasn't so much what he said but what he didn't. His voice was completely flat, like he'd shut the door on something unpleasant. It felt off, even though she couldn't put her finger on it. Kelley looked up at him, at once afraid and intrigued. She was curious, but to press might push him away and that was the last thing she wanted. Part of her wanted to hold his hand and help him as he'd helped her last night, even without knowing it. He had changed everything with his gentle touches and thorough loving. But another part begged her to leave it alone and not ruin this perfect day.

"Then let's go shopping. I'll spring for Candy Cane Fudge at the Creamery."

The dark cloud of his expression passed as she changed the subject. "That sounds good."

7

The last of the plastic packaging was in the garbage, the smell of cocoa came from the kitchen, and Kelley stood in the doorway to the living room, staring at her transformed house.

Evergreen boughs punctuated by red bows swooped from the loft railing, ending in a trail down the banister. A large bouquet of red poinsettias and white mums in a sleigh made a centerpiece on the pine coffee table. Cinnamon-scented candles glowed from a glass holder atop the mantle. A fired burned briskly in the fireplace, and their newly decorated tree stood proudly in the corner, a mass of twinkling lights and shining ornaments, a glorious white angel gracing the top. Kelley realized that for the first time ever, it looked like a home, not just a house. It was warm and welcoming.

In the kitchen, Mack turned from the stove, whisk in hand, completing the festive picture. "Cocoa's nearly done."

Even in here she and Mack had worked magic. Now her table was dressed in a bright red and green plaid cloth. Green napkins were rolled and arranged in a glass jar, almost like a bouquet. It was all so pretty and perfect, like something out of a magazine.

"It smells wonderful. And the house looks gorgeous. Thank you, Mack, for doing all of this with me. I don't remember the last time I had so much fun…"

She stammered at the end, unsure of how to put her feelings so that he understood, and yet without frightening him away. There'd been times today he'd been so open, so relaxed. And then other times he'd seemed somehow distant, more like an observer than a participant. She knew which she preferred—how could she make him see it?

He blindly turned off the burner and let the whisk sink into the creamy chocolate. His dark eyes touched on hers, and she wished he'd smile. If he smiled, she could tell what he was thinking. Her heart pounded as he crossed the kitchen to where she was standing.

"I did it because I wanted to." He reached out and took one of her hands in his. "Being with you has been fun. I don't remember the last time I was excited for Christmas. You did that, Kelley. Just you."

He paused, as if going to say something more, but his cell phone rang and he took it out of his back pocket. He looked at the number. "Do you mind?" he asked.

"No, go ahead." He'd been giving her a lot of his time lately; she understood he also had a business to run.

She sipped the cocoa while he disappeared into the living room to talk. His business was in the city. Frequently traveling. And hers was here, at Rocking H. With times getting tougher, she couldn't afford to hire more help. And she needed to keep the ranch profitable, to sustain them all. It seemed unrealistic to be swept away in a flight of fancy. Perhaps they'd both been getting caught up in the magic of Christmas. Maybe she should just tuck the memories of last night away like a Christmas present, something special and surprising and unexpected.

"Did you see what else I bought?" His phone call finished, his smooth voice interrupted her thoughts, and she bit her lip. He was smiling but there were new lines of strain around his eyes she hadn't seen before.

"No," she said weakly, and then he pointed up.

A sprig of mistletoe hung from the door frame, tied with a red ribbon.

She looked back down and into his eyes. And ceased caring about what would happen after Christmas day or all the reasons why she should play it cautious. For once in her life she was going to get caught up in the moment. If ever there were a season for it, it was Christmas. She put her hand on his cheek before standing up on tiptoe and kissing him.

He put his hands on the small of her back and drew her closer as their mouths, tongues meshed. He tasted like mint and chocolate from their fudge earlier. His body was a hard, impenetrable wall as she pressed against it, absorbing its warmth and strength. If she got no other gift for Christmas, having Mack's arms around her was enough. He'd taken her fears of the physical and erased them with his first kiss. He'd made her feel wanted and hadn't run away at the first opportunity. He murmured into her mouth and her pulse raced, fluttering frantically at her neck, wrist. This, just this, was enough.

"Mmmm," he murmured, pulling back just enough so that their lips parted. "Do you know how good you are at that?"

"Me?" She whispered it, their breaths mingling as they hovered at another kiss.

"Yeah, you," he replied.

She looked into his eyes, mesmerized by the tiny gold flecks around his pupils. "I haven't had much practice."

"If you improve, you're going to be the death of me, Miss Hughes." He grinned and a dimple appeared. "Come to think of it, maybe we'd better get started on your education. Practice does make perfect." And his mouth closed over hers again, slow and lingering.

A tiny bit of loneliness crept in even as her arms wrapped around his shoulders. What would happen after the holidays, when everything was put away? Would he disappear along with the bows and ribbons?

No, she refused to think of the new year and all the unknowns. She would not ruin it by thinking of things that hadn't even happened yet.

"As much as I would like to carry on this conversation upstairs, I have to go," he murmured, pressing a kiss to the tip of her nose. "Something's come up."

"Let it wait." She smiled up at him. "You deserve a day to yourself."

The lines around his eyes were back. "I wish," he murmured. "But I need to look after this."

"You could come back when you're done," she suggested. "We could watch a movie on TV."

His gaze fell to her mouth again, but then he exhaled. "I need some clean clothes. I wasn't actually expecting to spend the night last night."

Kelley had the silly urge to point out she had a washing machine. And a bathtub. The former which he could use and the latter which he could share, along with a healthy dose of bubbles. But the words stuck in her throat…it seemed so forward, so uncharacteristic of her. It wasn't something she could blithely suggest or seduce her way into. It just wasn't in her. So she backed off, knowing it was foolish to feel she'd been rejected but feeling it just the same.

"That's okay. I'm sure having your truck parked out front two mornings in a row would raise some eyebrows at the house."

She turned away, pretending to tend the cocoa on the stove. She took a spoon and tried skimming off the thin skin that had formed on the top.

He came over and touched her hand, guiding it and helping scoop the bit on to a saucer. "You should be thankful your family cares."

"I am. But I have a right to my privacy."

"Not everyone has a family like yours, Kelley."

Her lips dropped open at his sharp tone. "I know

that, too. Are we starting to argue? It feels like it and I don't know why."

"Don't you?"

The air hummed.

"No, I don't!" She grabbed the nearby ladle and started pouring the hot drink into mugs. She handed one to him. "Why don't you enlighten me?"

He put down his cup, reached over and took hers and put it down too. Then he grabbed her upper arms and made her face him.

"You have a family that loves you. That cares for you and wants to protect you. You are moving heaven and earth to make Christmas for them, and I envy that."

Her eyes widened.

"This is the first Christmas I've spent any time with anyone other than a business associate. I've been in many cities around the world, but this is the first time I've cut down a tree and decorated it. Having a family whose opinion matters isn't something you take for granted!"

"I don't!"

"You've got everything here, don't you see that? And still you want more."

His censure stung, and she was done with apologizing for wanting something other than a solitary life on the family ranch. Something for herself. "I suppose you're an open book, right? There are parts of you, Mack Dennison, that are one big question mark."

He backed away as if her arms were suddenly scalding hot and burning his hands. "You don't know what you're talking about."

"I did hit a nerve." She felt herself getting angry now. He'd kissed her and held her and made love to her. He understood everything, and yet nothing. So much of him was a mystery.

"What you told me this morning hardly fills in all the blanks, Mack. And I don't know why you're suddenly so angry at me. You told me in the motel room that wanting more saved your life. I think I understand why you said that now. But why is okay for *you* and not for *me*?"

"I didn't have what you have," he retorted.

"Your *last* store was the one you set up here, not your first. What were *you* running from?"

Mack decided to pick up his cocoa after all. He took one sip but it tasted bitter. He took the cocoa and dumped it down the sink.

He'd let himself get caught up in the Christmas fervor with her today. But that was just it. It was Christmas, a sentimental, holiday illusion. In the bright light of the new year, everything would be much clearer. She was getting caught up in the holiday, that was all. It did funny things to people.

"I wasn't running from anything. I was building a life for myself."

"Then why did you come back?"

The answer was so close to the tip of his tongue it scared him. He'd had no choice. It was why the house on the bluff would now be his home.

Did she truly know what today had meant? What a

leap it had been for a man like him? The last time he'd let himself need anyone was with Lissy, in London. He'd damn near bought her a ring. But the moment he'd told her the truth about his upbringing, the reason he was suddenly tied to Montana with invisible strings, he hadn't seemed nearly as attractive. He'd realized the links to his past were a liability. He'd spent that Christmas in a hotel in Los Angeles rather than in Lissy's flat as planned. And he'd vowed he'd never let himself need a woman again.

And as Kelley stared at him, he wanted to take away the hurt in her eyes and make her smile again. He was starting to seek her approval, wanting to please her, and the thought went a long way to cooling his heels.

"Let's just enjoy Christmas, okay? I don't want to argue with you. Not now."

He put a hand along her cheek, trying to soften her mutinous expression and failing. He had to get out of here now before he did something crazy, like tell her how he felt about her. He'd broken rules one and two, but three would stay in force. He couldn't be in love with her.

"I need to go now and look after this. I'll be back on Christmas Eve for final prep."

"That long." Her voice was like acid—he'd made her mad. Why did things have to get so complicated?

He laughed tightly, the sound thick with the undercurrents swirling in the room. "You've got everything you need in your fridge. Amelia's still doing dessert?"

"Yes, she is insistent she does the pies. It wouldn't be Christmas without her pies."

Another tradition he had no point of reference to. He felt like walls were closing in and he had to get away. But he couldn't. He would go straight from here to the one place he dreaded more than any on earth.

"Right. I'll see you then."

Guilt crawled along his spine. And yet he couldn't bring himself to tell her the truth. He leaned over and kissed her forehead. "Bye, Kelley."

He left her standing there in the kitchen, with a mug full of cold cocoa and a little piece of his heart left behind.

CHRISTMAS EVE DAWNED AS ALL CHRISTMAS EVES should: cheerfully bright, white, and crisp. When Kelley got out of bed, it was with a sense of excitement she hadn't had since she'd been a small child. Today Mack was coming back. She'd fix what had gone wrong between them. It was Christmas Eve! Anything was possible.

Today they were going to make ahead the orange salad and cranberry sauce. They would forget their harsh words and focus on having a merry Christmas.

She touched a finger to an angel ornament, remembering what he'd said when he'd bought it for her. That it reminded him of her. All she knew was that she wasn't ready for it to be over after tonight. She needed him to know how much he meant to her. And that meant sharing with him too.

She showered and dressed carefully, in low slung

jeans and a soft sweater than hugged her slim form more than she was used to. She pulled a small amount of hair back from each side of her face, holding it with a small clip, while the rest of her hair fell down her back. The new-found interest in her appearance was a revelation. She realized that with Mack, she didn't want to hide. She wanted him to see her. And she wanted him to like what he saw.

She pressed a hand to her nervous tummy as he arrived, carrying a bag with the fresh ingredients required for the day. "Good morning," he smiled, pushing his boots off with his toes and handing her the groceries, as if their harsh words had never happened. "And Merry Christmas."

The bubbles of excitement fizzed stronger as he dropped a light kiss on her lips. More than ever she was determined to prove to him that she could do this. That his faith in her hadn't been misplaced. But more than that, she wanted to show him how things could be between them. Not just today. Every day.

"Are you ready for your next lesson?"

"I put myself in the hands of the master."

"Well now. That's a dangerous spot to be in." He winked at her and she laughed. Perhaps she'd just imagined his darker mood of Sunday afternoon, for right now it was lighter than it had been all week. More than ever she wanted to tell him everything—about how he'd changed things for her, about how she wanted more time with him. It was a matter of waiting for the right moment. Maybe tonight, when it was just the two of them in front of the tree…

"A dangerous spot for you," she joked. "I know you. You won't be able to keep your hands off my turkey."

She put the bag on the counter, thrilled when his arms snaked around her waist. "I won't be able to keep my hands off of something," he agreed.

Kelley turned within the circle of his arms and looked up. He was smiling and teasing but there was something else lurking behind his eyes. She wished she knew what it was. "You're different today."

His arms tightened and his gaze dropped to her lips before moving back up. "I missed you, Kel."

"I missed you too." Her heartbeat quickened as he dropped a light kiss on her lips, then another. It was the closest he'd gotten to an admission of his feelings. But was it enough? Could they make it work beyond Christmas? She knew she wanted it to.

Mack's heart swelled at her words and he kissed her because he didn't know what to say. He had missed her. And in missing her, he'd discovered something very unpleasant. He needed her. And he didn't like needing anyone. He had to find a way to let her go, for both their sakes. But not today. He wasn't so cruel that he'd do it today.

He touched her nose with a finger. "Today is Christmas Eve. The final countdown to your culinary triumph. Should we get started? If we finish early…"

When everything was ready, Kelley wiped the last dish, looked around the kitchen with the cranberry sauce a ruby-red ribbon in a glass dish and the orange salad arranged prettily on a snowflake patterned plate. Tomorrow she'd prepare vegetables and turkey at the main house, and they'd all sit down to a holiday meal together. With one extra. She smiled to herself. The phone call from Boone today had been a surprise. It was all going to work out—for all of them. She just knew it.

"Well, let's hope the execution goes as well as the preparation," she said, standing back and brushing her hands down her apron. She untied it from around her waist and hung in over a chair. "Thank you, Mack. For everything. When I walked into your store…"

"I know," he replied. He stood in front of the counter, his hands in his pockets. The afternoon sun bathed him in light through the window above the sink. "I didn't expect you. I sure didn't expect any of this to happen."

How could she ever get through dinner, when she was dying inside, longing to tell him how she felt? She swallowed and gathered up some courage. "I was scared to death. I had to be to ask for help, you realize that, right? But I don't regret it, not for a moment. I hope you don't, either."

He came over to her then, and framed her face with his hands. "Kelley the stubborn. So determined." His smile was soft. "Is that what you think? That I regret it?"

She couldn't answer, so she shrugged.

"Making love to you had been in my head for days. Ever since the night in the motel room. Maybe even before then…maybe as far back as seeing you walk into my store, pretending to know what you were about."

She laughed, a soft, almost-sob. A sentimental Mack was a treat she hadn't expected. "I had no idea."

"I'm not sorry for anything that's happened the last week. Not one thing."

She took a deep breath and tilted her chin so she could look up at him. It was a sweet thing to say, so why did she get the feeling it was a first step to goodbye?

She rested her fingers on the waistband of his jeans. "That being the case…I was going to ask you. Do you want to stay tonight?"

She held her breath. *Please say yes.* She wanted to share Christmas with him. All of it. She'd never had a significant other to share holidays with and it was so much cozier with two. She wanted his face to be the first one she saw as dawn crept over the white hills. To know that she wasn't alone. To watch him over the rim of a coffee cup with the lit tree behind them. Simple things, but special ones.

"I'd love to, but I'm up due at the shelter, remember?" There was a trace of regret in his voice. She grabbed on to it.

"Come back when you're done. I'll leave the tree on and a fire burning."

"Why do you want me to, Kelley?"

"Because…because…" She stammered for a few moments. Why did she want him there? And it wasn't just about the sentimentality of the holiday, or not wanting to be alone. She knew that. It went deeper. So much deeper she could hardly breathe. The words sat on her tongue while she deliberated if she should say them or not. The differences between them, the secrets, vanished when he was like this with her. All that mattered was the way he touched her, spoke to her. And if she didn't say it now, she might not have another chance.

"Because Christmas is meant to be spent with people you love." Her words came out on a quiet whisper, yet they echoed to every corner of the room. "Don't you think, Mack?"

He backed away. "Kelley…"

"You have to know what this week has meant to me. And I need to tell you Mack, because being with you, it changed *everything*. More than you can imagine."

She sighed, knowing she wanted to do this but finding it unbearably difficult just the same. "I don't think you realize how much," she murmured. Her eyes captured his. "I need to tell you something, Mack, so you'll understand. But please…I need your arms around me when I do."

He hesitated a moment, but then took a step forward, holding out his hands. "Come here," he whispered, and she went into the safe circle of his arms.

He was warm and strong and all those things that had made her trust him in the first place. When she'd gathered strength from his embrace, she pulled back just a little. Close enough to feel the heat from his body, far enough away she could have the room to speak.

The kitchen smelled of spices and cranberries. Kelley knew that she would succeed in making a beautiful family dinner. It had been her goal, and yet it all seemed silly and trivial at this moment. His gaze darkened, held reservations but she expected that. She felt as though she were standing on the edge of something, and one small slip could ruin it all.

She reached up with trembling fingers and touched his cheek. "Being with you the other night changed something in me. I didn't think I'd ever be able to unfreeze enough to be with a man, Mack. But with you it was different. I saw you with Risky and I wondered if you were the one who would be gentle enough, understanding enough. And you were."

"I don't understand."

"When you told me about your childhood, I knew you'd understand. Oh Mack, you're not the only one with secrets. I've never told anyone about this. Not Gram, not Amelia…but I want you to know, Mack."

She gripped his hands, a lifeline to get her through it. She'd never once said the words out loud, not even to herself.

"I know you felt unloved and unwanted by your mom. But you're not, not by me. I want you to know how much you've given me. The truth is, when we graduated…"

Her throat closed over as images raced through her mind, followed by crippling fear. She could almost feel his hands again, hear the raspy sound of his mocking voice. Her breath quickened and she closed her eyes.

No. It was over and done. Wilcox had left Rebel Ridge a long time ago, and he no longer held any power over her. She replaced the images with the memory of lying in Mack's arms, feeling loved and cherished. Two solitary tears gathered at the corners of her eyes and squeezed out, rolling silently down her cheeks.

"Kelley." His voice was a hushed whisper, his fingers firm on hers. Reassuring.

"The truth is, on prom night I was raped, and I haven't been with a man since. Until you."

8

The words sent a rush of relief flooding through Kelley's body. It was cathartic, saying it out loud. Suddenly they didn't have the same power. Being with Mack had made it possible to move on. Just saying the words opened up new vistas for her. She wanted to see places, experience things. No more hiding away.

"What?" Mack's voice was filled with disbelief and stepped back, leaving her without the shelter of his arms. She shivered, feeling the sudden cold. She'd thought the hard part was over, but the euphoric release only lasted a minute. Explaining was going to be much more difficult than she imagined.

"It happened after the prom," she began, her voice wobbling a little. "I…I had a date for the dance, and I thought I was ready. So many of the other girls…and he was popular, and handsome…looking back now I think I just wanted to feel feminine, and pretty, and wanted.

Gram had taken me to buy a new dress and it was so beautiful."

She started to choke on the words and fought to regain control. "I was always the tomboy, you see."

"You hid behind boots and jackets and braids."

She nodded, relieved he understood. "When he asked me out, I went. I didn't know I was being used. But at the last minute... I changed my mind. But he didn't care. We weren't at the party everyone had gone to. Instead we went to a cabin out back of their spread. It was small and dark and I heard the click of the door locking. I...I can still hear it in my nightmares. I asked to leave but then he grabbed me and..."

The lip quivered uncontrollably now as tears swelled over her bottom lashes. She could still feel the hands that had seemed to be everywhere at once and her stomach churned. "I should have fought him off, right?" Her voice sounded small and far away. "I didn't fight him, and I should have."

"He raped you." The words came out dull, dead. Final.

She shrugged pitifully. "I said no, but he didn't like that. In the end...oh Mack," she pleaded. "In the end... It was horrible and heartbreaking. Even now, I hate being in dark places. The motel room during the blizzard was awful."

MACK STARED AT HER, TEARS STAINING HER CHEEKS AND her lips quivering. Never had he expected this. He'd known she was innocent; not a virgin obviously but her sweetness had said it all. But dammit, what was he supposed to do with *this*? The magnitude of it all crashed down on Mack and he had no idea what to say, how to act. If only she'd said something. Dear Lord, he'd kissed her in that room, sensed she was nervous, but had never imagined something like this. If he'd known, he would never have left her to sit through the storm all alone.

"I'm not sure how…I mean… why me?"

She sent him a tenuous smile. "You're wonderful, that's why. Being with you was…a revelation. I wasn't afraid. I trusted you. I knew after seeing you with Risky that you'd be gentle and kind and…"

Suddenly she broke off and her face flamed.

The magnitude sunk in and Mack knew exactly what he'd done. He'd gone and seduced a woman completely unprepared for it. It hadn't been a level playing field. And he'd stupidly told himself he was in control but the truth was, *he'd* needed *her*. And he'd taken her without any thought as to what affect it would have. He rubbed a hand over his face.

That made him a selfish bastard. Careless. He'd ignored the signs. The way she'd been timid, innocent, the way she'd been afraid in the motel room…he'd thought only of himself.

Because he needed her.

And it scared him to death.

"Why now? Why tell me now?"

Tears glimmered on her cheeks and he felt about two inches tall.

"Because I fell in love with you. Because you trusted me and I thought I could trust you."

His breath came out in a whoosh. How could he possibly tell her that he'd only talked about his childhood in an effort to put distance between them? And that it had the opposite effect? He paced to the tree, staring at the lights that all seemed to blur together.

He felt like he was drowning and needed a life preserver. All he could think about was how she must have been terrified. Thinking about another man's—no, boy's—hands on her skin when she'd said no. It damn near broke his heart. What must it have taken for her to let him…knowing what had come before…

He hung his head, letting out a raw breath. There were things she didn't know. She'd been through enough. How could he possibly burden her any further with his own problems? They certainly weren't going away. She was just embarking on her life, making all these self-discoveries. And he was the one tied down.

"You said love," he whispered hoarsely. "Love is a word that gets thrown around far too often, and when it's convenient."

Her eyes took on a wounded look. "You don't believe me."

He had to turn away. He'd had no agenda. He'd said he'd help her. He'd agreed to let her hire him. He'd even trusted her with the story of his mother. How had it ever come to this?

She was really crying now, and it killed him to see her red-rimmed eyes. He'd trusted her. He needed her.

He'd fallen in love with her. All three rules broken. It was a complete disaster. She deserved better than him. She was ready to spread her wings. He'd only slow her down.

"I can't do this," he said, swallowing thickly against the knot of denial. "There are things…" He stopped just short of saying the words. His jaw tightened. "You don't need me, Kelley. You need someone who can put you first."

"And you can't?"

He closed his eyes. What got him most was that he wanted to believe her, and knowing it caused that slow, sick turning he recognized as dying hope. Just like he'd wanted to believe the others. Like he'd believed his mother every time a promise had been made. Like he'd believed Lissy when she'd said the words. But at the end of the day, none of them stayed.

And then a cowgirl in a Christmas crisis had shown up at his shop and turned everything upside down. And he knew that to let himself hope with her was different. He'd given her his heart without even realizing it. And if he told her, and then lost her…he was pretty damn sure this time he wouldn't bounce back.

He heard her sniff and was filled with self-loathing. She only thought she felt this way. In time she'd realize he wasn't right for her. And yet, somehow the little boy inside still longed to hear the words.

"What do you want, Kelley?" He said the words slowly, testing them out. "Because it's more than a turkey and a Christmas tree. What do you see happening between us?"

· · ·

KELLEY GATHERED WHAT LITTLE BIT OF COURAGE SHE had left around her. This wasn't how she'd planned it to go. She'd wanted his arms around her, comforting words of love and support. She'd wanted to tell him how she felt, and she'd hoped he would feel the same way. Instead she was faced with a cold stranger, and she did the only thing she knew how to do. She couldn't let herself fall apart again, even though she was quaking on the edge of it. She'd come too far.

She tried to cover her hurt with ice. "If you think I asked you to stay out of some misplaced obligation, you're perfectly mistaken. I asked you because I thought we shared something special, and that you might want to share your first 'real' Christmas with me."

"If it's because of what I told you and…"

She couldn't let him finish. She had to press forward. "Did you think what we shared was part of your payment? Or that I did it out of what, misplaced pity? Or worse, that I *used* you?" This wasn't about hiring him or feeling sorry for a poor, misused boy. It was because of the man he'd become. Why couldn't he see that?

At his lack of response, she tilted her chin. "I thought you thought more of me than that. I thought you saw me for *me*."

"I do," he uttered, his deep voice hoarse as he stood before the tree they'd decorated together. "Believe me, Kelley, what you think are feelings now aren't real. One day you'll turn around and I'll be *that guy* that helped you get over *that time*."

"Do you really think so little of me?" Her mouth dropped open in dismay. "Of yourself?"

"No! And…" He paused. Sighed. "This was never part of the plan. And now you tell me you were…" he couldn't make himself say the word again, "and I feel like someone sucker punched me."

His eyes darkened with anguish. "I can't get past the picture of his hands on you." He took a shuddering breath. "I'm angry…and I'm feeling helpless. And those are two emotions I've had to work very hard to overcome."

It was becoming clear he couldn't handle the truth. She'd been a fool to think he could. This was exactly why she hadn't told him before. "Are you saying you don't want to see me after today?"

"I got caught up in the moment with you. I wanted a real Christmas and I fell for it all. But that's not what's real. Life isn't this way every day—all perfect and pretty and goodwill towards men. Sometimes it's ugly and lonely."

"You are a coward."

THE WORDS CAME OUT OF HER MOUTH IN AN IMPULSIVE, hurtful rush and Mack recoiled against the blow. It was like she'd driven a knife between his ribs, cutting off his air. He'd wanted desperately to be wrong. For her to tell him he'd been wrong. But he deserved it. Every single bit. He could turn it around and around all he wanted, use her eleventh hour revelation as an excuse, but the truth was he would only hurt her and ending it now would be doing her a favor. He couldn't ask her to take him on. Not with everything he had to deal with these days.

"You're right. I am a coward."

Her eyes glittered as her back straightened. There was none of the timidity, none of the self-consciousness he'd seen. In its place was a strength that was beautiful to behold, even as her words of truth cut into him like knives.

"You, Mack, are lying to yourself. So what if you helped me move past what was holding me back? That doesn't mean it was meaningless." She went to him and touched his arm. He looked down at her fingers but resisted the urge to cover them with his own. Something was happening here, something bigger than asking him to spend Christmas. Something he couldn't face.

"Kelley," he began, but she cut him off.

"In fact, I think the only reason it did work was because it *wasn't* meaningless. I believe in my heart it could only have been with *you*. And if knowing it makes you scared, well join the club. It frightens the hell out of me. I'll be damned if I'll run away from it. You made me love you. But you go ahead and be a coward."

She went to her purse and took out a check. "Here you go. Paid in full. Just like we agreed."

She opened his palm and put the paper in it, then closed his fingers over top. She turned away and disappeared into the kitchen.

For a few moments he thought about going after her. But then he remembered the phone call on Sunday, knew where he'd be tomorrow afternoon. This was for the best. He quietly put on his things, tucking the check back into her purse as he went out the door.

KELLEY SAT AT THE KITCHEN TABLE, HER HANDS FOLDED in front of her. He hadn't come back. Hadn't called. She missed him. All week she'd imagined having him beside her tonight. She'd imagined giving him the tiny present she'd picked up on impulse as they sat next to the tree. She had wanted to put on the new dress she'd bought and fix her hair and feel beautiful.

Instead, she'd had a good cry, and then gone upstairs and changed into a pair of soft pajamas. Tomorrow she'd put on a merry face and do the family Christmas.

For tonight, she was just miserable.

She got up and made a pot of coffee. The familiar smell of Mack's special grind reminded her of the morning she'd awakened with him sitting on the side of the bed. She missed him with a loneliness so unfamiliar and sharp that she had a hard time breathing. Now Boone was coming back, and Amelia was going to have her chance at happiness. Kelley had thought it was going to work out for all of them. And while she was happy for her sister, it was a stark reminder of how she'd come so close and lost.

She took her coffee and turned on the television. It was all Christmas programming—the day simply could not be ignored. She left it on White Christmas, but only half paid attention to Bing Crosby and Rosemary Clooney crooning at each other. She thought of Mack, earlier tonight, serving dinner to the homeless. Why hadn't she volunteered to go with him when he'd first told her? Would it have made a difference in the end?

In a matter of minutes, it would be Christmas day. And despite all her planning, she was alone.

The lights on the tree glittered, reflecting off the foil-wrapped gift that lay beneath the branches. Inside was a set of ornaments in the shape of kitchen utensils. She'd hoped that tonight they could put them on the tree together. Kneeling down, she picked up the box and ran her hand over the paper, feeling the awful urge to cry. She'd come out from beneath the heavy mantle of her hurts, but he hadn't. Her heart ached for the boy who had been so lonely. A man who wouldn't—couldn't —trust.

A man who didn't love her. Who would rather leave than let himself give into love—to be loved.

The knock on the door startled her out of her musings. She pressed a hand to her heart, her first thought that it might be Mack. She stood upright and let out a breath, surprised that the hope hit her so hard. It was probably just Amelia with some last-minute thought about tomorrow's dinner.

She opened the door and there he was.

His breath made a cloud in the bitter night as a few flakes of snow fluttered beyond the verandah. His hands were in his jacket pockets, the sheepskin collar turned up against the cold.

The frigid air snuck into the house through the open door as seconds passed.

"I missed you," he said finally.

A tiny glimmer of hope kindled. He was here. She wouldn't risk him leaving again; tonight there could be nothing but absolute truth.

"I missed you too."

"And I want to be with you," he said, his dark eyes holding hers captive. "I love you, Kelley."

The glimmer burst into flame as he stepped forward, surrounded her with his arms, kicking the door shut behind him. For the moment nothing else mattered... she was in his arms again. He was there, for her. Everything else melted away.

"I love you too, Mack."

He put her down, cradled her cheekbones with his thumbs. "You mean it? Even after everything I said today?"

"Yes, I do."

He dipped his head and touched his lips to hers, gently, reverently. "I'm sorry about this afternoon," he whispered, dotting light kisses on her cheeks. "Nothing came out right."

She put her arms around him and rested her head on his wide shoulder. The fabric of his coat was still cold from outside and she inhaled the leathery scent of winter mixed with the clean cologne she now knew was simply *Mack*. "Keep going," she said softly. "You're doing okay so far."

He laughed, a low, sexy rumble that somehow turned the world right again. "Look at you," he marveled, standing back and holding her hands out.

She belatedly realized she was in cream colored flannel pajamas, and that she'd done nothing with her hair since taking it out of the clip. "Oh, don't look at me! I'm a mess!"

"You're beautiful. All cream and pink and…your hair is down." He let go of her hands and reached out, touching a golden strand. "I love it when your hair is down."

Tears stung her eyelids. "Thank you."

Kelley closed her eyes. He was here. Really here. "I missed you so much. I didn't think you were coming back."

"I didn't either. Until I realized I wanted to stop running." He led her to the sofa, and they sat down. "I've been running for so long I'm not sure I know how to do anything else."

She squeezed his hand. "That's a start."

"Why did you come to *me?*" he asked at last. "Why did you ask me for help?"

"I think I was just meant to be there, at that time, in that place. And there you were. The answer to my problems, and I didn't even know it."

He nodded slowly. Kelley watched him struggle with something and her heart softened even more. "What about you, then? Why did you agree?"

"I saw you were trying to give. To give something of yourself to make it easier for the family you obviously love. I never had a Christmas with decorated trees or dinners or presents. I never saw one where a family loved each other enough to go the extra mile. What you were doing—it was selfless."

He looked down at their fingers. "You were like that with me, too. And I pushed you away. You deserve better than me," he whispered hoarsely. "You deserve more than the kid of an alcoholic that couldn't have cared less whether her son lived or died, a child who didn't matter."

"You can't turn back the clock. You can't pretend it didn't happen. You do matter. To so many people. To me. Oh Mack, I know." Her lip quivered but she pressed on, knowing he had to understand exactly how she felt. "You know why Mack's Kitchen works for you? Because you can still be on the outside looking in. And as scary as that is, it's not nearly as scary as dealing with it. Just like me being with a man was too frightening to think about. Until you. You took my fears away."

Mack turned away first, faced the Christmas tree. She was right, he knew it.

"You give other people what you want for yourself, but are too afraid to believe in it." She rubbed a hand between his shoulder blades as he nodded. He felt the warmth even through his heavy coat. He'd gone to the shelter this afternoon, still angry and confused. But as he'd served a turkey dinner to those without homes, his thoughts were always with Kelley. The pleasure he normally felt in helping out was soured. And he'd realized in a very painful way that the rest of his life was destined to be the same if he didn't stop tap-dancing around the facts and just be honest. He needed her. And it was okay.

"When I was home alone tonight, I realized that the work was just a substitute for happiness. I went to the shelter but the joy of helping was gone from it. Because you are my joy. I had you and I lost you."

He looked into her eyes. They were so beautiful, hazel with the green flecks reflected by the mellow glow from the tree. "And then a couple came in. They had nothing. Their clothes were threadbare, their faces wrinkled. But they were holding hands. Her hands were so shaky." He swallowed as he recalled the way the woman's fingers had trembled as she'd reached for her plate.

"They took their dinner and sat together, and he reached over and buttered her roll. Such a small gesture, but she smiled at him and I knew. He will always be there for her, no matter what. It's you, Kelley. It's you I need." He leaned forward, squeezed her hand has he emphasized, "*Just you*."

"Oh, Mack…"

"I was afraid. Afraid to trust in you, believe in you. But more than that…I was afraid to believe in myself. I set up those walls to protect myself because loving you made me vulnerable. Only it doesn't work without you."

But there was more he needed to say, to explain. He should have been truthful with her all along. He should have trusted her the way she'd trusted him. "So now I have to be completely honest."

He paused, tempted to stare at his hands but knew he had to face this dead on. He had to trust her. They'd come this far. "Tomorrow at the rehab center…" He swallowed. He could do this. "It's not just volunteering. I go to see my mother."

Kelley gasped, her eyes darting to his. Of all the things he could have said, he knew she hadn't expected this, and guilt snaked through him once more.

"Don't look at me that way," he said. "I know I should have told you."

"I thought you didn't know where your mother was."

"I didn't want to have to explain." He ran his hands through his hair. "And her body *is* there, Kel, but it's broken. And I don't know where her mind is. She left after high school, but I never heard from her again. Until I got a call that she was in hospital, and she'd listed me as her next of kin. She'd been drinking. She'd had an accident. The damage was permanent. She can't tell me from one of the orderlies."

She reached out and covered his hand with hers. "Oh Mack. How horrible. For both of you."

He blinked against the compassion in her voice. "It's why I finally came back, you know. At least this way I can be closer to her. Someone has to pay her bills. I don't want her in some dingy room without a window."

"I'm so sorry. I can only imagine that growing up you must have wished for things to change. And that with her accident…"

"Yes. There's no chance of it now. Maybe I should hate her for my childhood, but…"

"But she's your mother." She smiled softly, rubbing her thumb over the top of his hand. "And you still care about her and want to look after her."

He nodded, fighting back emotion. She understood. He wished he'd trusted her enough in the beginning to tell her. "The phone call the other day—that was the nurse on duty. My mother asked for me. That's the first time it's happened since the accident. But by the time I got there, she was gone again. And I was angry. I had let myself hope again."

"Of course you did." Kelley smiled. "A part of you always wanted to believe."

His fingers squeezed hers. "The last woman I told was two years ago. Our relationship ended very abruptly. I was afraid to tell anyone again, afraid to care so much about someone that it mattered."

"What changed your mind?"

He raised his hand and ran it down her hair. The tree lights glimmered off it. She was his angel, he realized. His everyday angel. Not just one for Christmas Eve or bringing out on holidays. She was the kind of woman who was strong enough to be there day in and day out. He twisted a few strands of her hair between his fingers. "You."

"Me?"

He smiled into her surprised face. "Yes, you. The weight's heavy, Kelley. And I realized that you had put your faith in me when you told me about your rape. And if you were willing to trust me with something so painful, then I could trust you. I just needed to admit it to myself."

Kelley looked down at their joined hands. It was like a world opened up to her, one with more colors and facets than she even knew existed. It was enough that he asked. "You don't have to go through it alone, Mack."

His breath came out with a whoosh as he pulled her close. "I spent a lot of Christmases looking for a miracle," he said into her hair. "And it was right here all along."

Tears clogged in her throat as her fingers dug into his back. "Right back at you," she whispered. And when she finally eased her grip on him, he kissed her. Again. And again. And once more, like he was afraid she'd disappear from his embrace.

She got up from the sofa and went to the tree, picking up the present she'd bought for him. "Here," she said, holding it out. "It's not much. But when I saw it…"

He undid the ribbon and wrapping, grinning at the display of miniature utensils inside. "For your tree."

"For our tree," she corrected. He stood, handed her a tiny potato masher sporting holly on the handle and tied with gold ribbon. "Here. You should hang the first one."

Together they hung the ornaments, and then stood back to admire the tree.

"I realized something tonight," she whispered, leaning back into the shelter of his arms. The fire had burned down, leaving only glowing embers. "The truth is I've hidden behind this ranch for so long I don't think I realized I was even doing it. It was my one thing, you know. And I held on to it tight."

"And now you're letting go?"

"I didn't put enough faith in people either. Amelia deserved more of it. And now…well, her happy ending is on his way here. Things are going to change around Rocking H. I don't have to hold onto it with both hands."

"You're giving up the ranch?"

She laughed. "Not completely. Maybe I can hang on

with one hand?" She leaned back so she could look up at him. "And hang on to someone else with the other?"

"I like that idea. As long as I'm the someone else."

"You don't see any other sexy chefs around here, do you?"

He laughed. "There'd better not be. In any case, I'm glad to hear it. Because I was kind of hoping that I could pull you away for a few days."

She smiled then, a soft smile filled with sweetness. "Where are we going?"

"How does Washington sound? I have a short trip there for work in the new year. It's not very glamorous… but it is convenient."

She slid closer to him, felt his arm tighten her, warm and secure. "It works for me. As long as you're there."

"And after that…I'll take you anywhere you want to go. London. Paris. Rome."

The thought was so big she could barely comprehend it. But while she'd always felt the need to see things, there was something that suddenly mattered more.

"I got you something too," he said casually.

"You did?"

He went over to his jacket and fumbled in the pocket. When he came back, he held up a sprig of mistletoe.

"It worked once before…"

She stepped forward and placed her hands on his chest. "Powerful stuff, that mistletoe." And she kissed him as he held the mistletoe above their heads.

When she stepped back, breathless, he smiled, like he had a secret.

"What?"

"It worked. Mistletoe is supposed to be a plant of truce. Even among lovers."

"You didn't think you needed reinforcements, did you? Not that I'm complaining."

"Now, about that travel. Paris. London. Rome," he continued thoughtfully, "any of those places would be wonderful for a honeymoon."

She put a hand to her chest. "A honeymoon!"

"Yes, a honeymoon." He lowered the mistletoe and she saw something dangling from the center of the clump. "Oh…."

It was a ring. Not a traditional engagement ring encrusted with diamonds, but a wide white gold band with an inlaid filigree design. Tiny diamonds winked from within the setting. She couldn't have picked anything more beautiful.

"I left the shelter and saw it in the store window. They were just closing up, but when I explained…" He unfasted the ring from its anchor. "I thought it would suit you for everyday, even when you were working. I didn't want to get you a ring you could only wear on special occasions." He slid it off the ribbon and poised it at the tip of her finger. "An everyday ring, for my everyday miracle."

She blinked rapidly as he looked down at her, so earnest, his dark eyes so full of love. For her.

"Will you marry me, Kelley? We can live here if you want…I know you like being close to your family.

Although the house is almost done and would be much bigger for our family. If you want babies. But it's your choice."

The tears that clogged her throat earlier returned, making it impossible to speak. After a life of always doing what was expected, to be given a choice was a glorious revelation. The horizons were bright and wide. And Mack would be beside her.

"Yes." She found her voice. "Yes, I will marry you. And we can live anywhere as long as we can fill it with babies. If that's what *you* want."

"I want," he confirmed.

The clock chimed the hour and she sighed. "Merry Christmas, Mack."

"Merry Christmas, sweetheart."

EPILOGUE

Kelley carried the turkey to the table on Great Grandma Hughes' ivory platter. Dishes glittered on the pristine white tablecloth; on a side table a tray of asparagus puffs was down to crumbs and the bottle of champagne Mack had brought nearly at the bottom. She caught Mack's gaze as he talked with Boone; his eyes twinkled back at her. Jesse knelt on the floor with his new train set while Ruby sat in her rocker, overseeing the locomotive's progress on the track. Amelia helped bring out the last of the dishes and for a moment the two sisters looked over their family.

"It's a picture, isn't it?" Kelley spoke softly, looking at her sister's beaming face. She smoothed the red and green apron that was protecting her new dress. "Everyone together. Gram hale and hearty, Jesse so happy. And you too. I'm so happy for you, sis." She reached down and squeezed Amelia's hand.

"It worked out," her sister said simply, but the smile that had been on her face since this morning had yet to fade. "And you look beautiful. A dress, and makeup. And did you hot roller your hair?"

Kelley felt a blush rise to her cheeks. She had put in extra effort this morning. It was an important morning. And she and Mack had decided together to wait for the right time to share their news.

"Let's call them all to the table," Kelley suggested, and left the task to Amelia, watching as her sister rounded up the family with motherly efficiency. She swallowed against the emotion rising in her throat. To think that such a short time ago, things had been so different. Now Boone was here, and they were going to join forces with the neighboring ranch he'd bought. As they all took their places around the table, Kelley slid the ring out of her apron pocket and back on to her finger, where it belonged.

"Gram? Will you do the honors?"

Ruby's voice rang out, strong and clear as she gave the simple, but heartfelt blessing. "Lord, thank you for this blessed holiday, for health, happiness, and bringing all of us together. Amen."

Kelley cleared her throat as the five bowed heads raised. "Well…" she gave a little laugh. "Before our professional carves the turkey, I have an announcement to make."

She got to her feet, feeling five other pairs of eyes on her. "First, my big sister welcome-to-the-family to Boone. I've never seen Jesse so happy or my sister so radiant." Boone and Amelia smiled at each other and Kelley felt the warmth of their love clear to her toes. "I was pretty happy to hear you were on your way back to these parts, Gifford. Welcome home."

Boone stood and came around the table to give her a hug. As he did, her ring sparkled on her left hand and Amelia gave a gasp.

"Kelley?"

She stepped back from Boone's embrace, and reached down to her right to take Mack's hand.

"Oh yes, I nearly forgot!" She laughed, knowing something so wonderful could never have slipped her mind. She gazed down into Mack's eyes. She would never tire of seeing that look there, just for her. "Mack proposed last night, and I accepted."

There was a general scrape of chairs against floor as they were pushed back, squeals of excitement and congratulations echoing through the room. Amelia rushed forward to hug her sister, Boone and Mack shook hands, and Gram came forward to give each and every one of them a hug while she dabbed at her eyes with a red and white handkerchief. "It's about time we had some menfolk around here," she announced.

When the hubbub quieted, Mack presided over the turkey while bowls were passed, and plates filled. Everything had turned out just right; Kelley had cooked a beautiful dinner with only the slightest input from Mack, who seemed reluctant to let her out of his sight. As Kelley ate, she listened to the chatter around her...two more places set this year, twice the happiness. What would next year bring?

But Jesse was being unusually quiet and she wrinkled

her brow. He'd wanted a father so desperately. What could be wrong?

"Jesse?"

"Yes, Aunt Kelley?"

"You okay sweetheart? You're awfully quiet."

He shrugged. "Just thinkin'."

She hid a smile behind her finger. "Thinkin' about what?"

Forks paused as everyone seemed interested in his answer.

"Well," he said, thoughtfully scooping up a helping of potato, "I was just wondering. Does this mean I'm gonna have a Daddy *and* an Uncle too?"

Her hand slid away from her mouth and she couldn't hold back the smile at the innocent question.

"Yes, Jesse, that's exactly what it means. Is that okay?"

His eyes widened, a gorgeous picture of boyish wonderment. "Oh yeah, it's okay."

He leaned over and tugged at Ruby's sleeve. "Hey, Grandma?" he whispered, just loud enough so everyone could hear.

"Yes, Jesse?"

"You were right, Grandma. About Santa."

Kelley's eyes stung with happy tears as she laughed. It was like a little miracle had suddenly happened right here at Rocking H. And as she took Mack's hand under the table, she understood that sometimes all you really needed to do was just believe.

ABOUT THE AUTHOR

While bestselling author Donna Alward was busy studying Austen, Eliot and Shakespeare, she was also losing herself in the breathtaking stories created by romance novelists like LaVyrle Spencer and Judith McNaught. Several years after completing her degree she decided to write a romance of her own and it was true love! Five years and ten manuscripts later she sold her first book and launched a new career. While her heartwarming stories of love, hope, and homecoming have been translated into several languages, hit bestseller lists and won awards, her very favorite thing is when she hears from happy readers.

Donna lives on Canada's east coast. When she's not writing she enjoys reading (of course!), knitting, gardening, cooking…and is a Masterpiece addict. You can visit her on the web at www.DonnaAlward.com and join her mailing list at www.DonnaAlward.com/newsletter .

Turn the page for a sample of another *Cowboy Collection* title, *The Cowboy's Bride!*

THE COWBOY'S BRIDE

Chapter One

"Miss? Wake up. Can you hear me?"

The deep voice came first, then Alex's vision gradually started to clear.

"Oh, thank God. Are you all right?"

Alex's eyes followed the sound of the voice as she looked up, dazed. Trying hard to focus, she found herself staring into the most beautiful set of brown eyes she'd ever seen. They were stunning, dark brown with golden flecks throughout, large and thickly lashed.

Men shouldn't have eyes that pretty, she thought irrationally, realizing with a jolt that she was captured in the arms of the eyes' owner.

"Oh, goodness!"

The eyes crinkled at the corners at her exclamation and she felt his hands on her arm and behind her back, helping her to rise.

"Slowly now. You fainted."

Really? I hadn't noticed. I was too busy being unconscious.
She bit back the sarcastic retort when she saw the
genuine concern in his eyes. He even made sure she was
standing firmly on her feet before releasing her—and
then stayed close, as if he didn't quite trust her to
remain steady.

He would have fainted, too, in her condition and
with this heat…and the lack of air conditioning in the
convenience store hadn't helped much, either.

"I'm so sorry," she blustered, brushing off her pants
and avoiding his eyes. It had only taken a moment, but
she could see him completely in her mind. Not just the
eyes, but thick, luscious black hair, just long enough to
sink your fingers into and slightly ragged at the edges.
Crisply etched lips and a large frame in a grey suit.

Someone who looked like him was so far departed
from her world it was laughable, and she avoided his
eyes from simple embarrassment. She stared instead at
his shoes…shiny, brown leather ones without a smudge
of dirt or a blemish. A businessman's shoes.

"No need to be sorry. Are you sure you're all right?"

She bent to retrieve her bag and purse. The first
time she'd bent to retrieve her dropped crackers, everything had spun and then turned black. This time she
gripped the bench for support, just in case. To her
dismay she realized that she'd spilled her apple juice and
it was running down a crack in the sidewalk. She folded
the top over on the paper bag, picked up the juice bottle
and looked around for a recycle receptacle.

"I'm fine," she said, finally looking him in the face.
Her heart skipped a beat at the worry she saw there. It

had been a long time since anyone had been concerned over her. He was a complete stranger, yet his worry was clear in the wrinkle between his brows. Gratitude washed over her for his gallantry. "I haven't even thanked you for catching me."

"You turned white as a sheet."

She chanced a quick look around. Any passers-by that had seen her little episode were gone, and now people went about their business, not paying any attention to them whatsoever. Another face in the crowd, that was all she was. Yet this man, Mr. GQ... had seen her distress and had come to her assistance.

"I'm fine. Thanks for your help. I'm just going to sit a moment." She coolly dismissed him; his duty was discharged.

Solicitously he stepped back to let her by, and once she sat, surprised her by seating himself as well. "Do you need a doctor?"

Alex laughed. Oh, she did, but a doctor couldn't cure what was wrong with her. "No."

The answer was definitive. By the way his shoulders straightened, she knew he got the message loud and clear. Briefly she felt guilty for being blunt, so she offered a paltry, "But thanks again, Mr...."

"Madsen. Connor Madsen." He held out his hand, undeterred, inviting her to introduce herself.

She took his hand in hers. It was warm and solid and a little rough. Not a banker's hands, as she'd thought. Working hands. Solid hands.

"Alex."

"Just Alex?"

His eyes were boring into her and she stared straight ahead at the office building across the street.

"Yes. Just Alex."

It wouldn't do to encourage him. In the early June heat, her t-shirt clung to her, the hem on the sleeves heavy on her arms and the fabric pulling uncomfortably across her breasts. And what had possessed her to wear jeans today, of all things? Apparently it wasn't that uncommon for such a heat wave this early in summer, but for her, the temperature did nothing but compound the light-headedness and nausea.

Necessity had forced her wardrobe choice, plain and simple. Her shorts weren't comfortable anymore and at least in her jeans she could breathe. As silence fell, thick and awkward between them, the world threatened to tilt again. The feeling slowly passed as she took slow, deep breaths. "For the love of Mike," she mumbled.

He laughed, a full-throated masculine sound that sent queer waves through her stomach. "So, just Alex. Intriguing name."

"Probably." She couldn't believe he was still here. After all, beyond the first fuzzy moment that she'd succumbed to his arms, she hadn't encouraged him at all. His attempt at polite conversation about her name had done nothing but awaken an all too familiar sadness, the heavy weight of regret every time she thought of her parents. "My full name is Alexis MacKenzie Grayson."

"That's quite a name for a small thing like you." His eyes were warm on her and he twisted, angling himself towards her and bending a knee.

"Alex for Graham Bell and MacKenzie for the Prime Minister, you know? You planning on using it for the paramedics later? In case I faint again?"

He chuckled and shook his head. "You look much better, thank goodness. But you spilled your juice. Can I get you something else cool to drink?" His eyes wandered to the convenience store behind them. "Perhaps a slurpee."

Her stomach rolled at the thought of the sugary sweet, slushy drinks. Every teenager in a ten-block radius had been buying slurpees today, and the very thought of them had Alex's tummy performing a slow, sickening lurch. She pressed her lips together.

"Or are you hungry? There's a hotdog cart down the street."

She stood, desperately trying to get some fresh air while exorcising the thought of greasy hotdogs from her mind. But she rose too quickly, her blood pressure dipped, and she saw grey and black shapes behind her eyes once again.

His arms were there to steady her, and she dropped her paper bag to the ground, the contents falling out as they hit the concrete.

His fingers were firm on her wrist as he helped her sit back down. "Put your head between your legs," he demanded quietly, and for some reason she obeyed.

Alex avoided his eyes as she sat back up moments later. "Sorry about that," she mumbled, completely mortified at the awkward silence that fell between them like a ton weight. This had to be an all-time low. Blacking out not once, but twice, in front of her own personal Knight in Shining Armor. And wasn't he annoying, this Mr. Perfect Chivalry, sitting there calm as you please.

She expected him to mumble his apologies and hurry away. Instead he knelt and began picking up what she'd dumped on the ground in her haste.

Oh God. Her humiliation was complete as he paused, his hand on the plastic bottle of pre-natal vitamins. His eyes darted up, caught hers. In them she saw sudden understanding. Now, of course, it all made sense. At least it made sense to *him*. She was still trying to assimilate everything.

"Congratulations."

Her smile was weak. He couldn't know. Couldn't know how her life had been turned completely upside down with a three-minute test only a few short weeks ago.

"Thank you."

He watched her carefully as he sat again on the bench. "You don't sound happy. Unplanned?"

She should end this conversation right here and now. He was, after all, a complete stranger.

"That's none of your business."

He had no cause to know her personal troubles. It was her problem. And she'd solve it. Somehow.

"I beg your pardon. I was only trying to help."

She grabbed the vitamins and shoved them into her purse. "I didn't ask for your help."

The pause was so long her scalp tingled under his scrutiny.

"No, you didn't. But I offer it anyway."

And who else was going to step up and give her a hand? She was alone, nearly destitute, and pregnant. She had no one waiting for her at home. *Home*, she thought sardonically. Now there was an idea. She hadn't had a real home in a long time…too long. Five years, to be exact. Five years was a long time to be at loose ends.

At present she was sleeping on the floor of a friend of a friend. Her back protested every morning, but it was the best she could do for now. She'd find a way, though, she thought with a small smile. She always did and had since being left alone and without a penny to her name at eighteen.

Connor was a friendly face and also the first person who actually seemed to care. Perhaps that was why she made the conscious choice to answer his question.

"Yes, this baby was unplanned. Very."

"And the father?"

She looked out over the bustling street. "Not in the picture."

He studied her for a few moments before replying, "So you're alone."

"Utterly and completely." Despair trickled through in her voice and she shored herself up. No sense dwelling on what couldn't be changed. Her voice was again strong and sure as she continued, "But I'll manage. I always do."

Connor leaned forward, resting his elbows on his knees. "Surely your family will help you."

"I have no family," she replied flatly, discouraging any further discussion of *that* topic. She had no one. Loneliness crept in, cold and heavy. Not one soul.

Anyone she'd truly cared about in the world was gone. Sometimes she almost forgot, but now, faced with a pregnancy and no prospects, she'd never felt more isolated.

After a long silence, he spoke again. "Are you feeling better? Would you like some tea or something?" He smiled at her, friendly, and her heart gave a little foreign twist at this complete stranger's obvious caring and generosity.

"You don't need to feel obligated. I'm fine now."

"Humor me. You're still a bit pale and it would make *me* feel better."

It was a lifeline to hold on to. It wasn't like her life was a revolving door of social invitations. "Tea might be nice, I guess."

She looped her purse over her shoulder. "So where are we off to, Connor Madsen?"

"There's a little place around the next corner."

She chuckled a little. "You use that line often?"

"I don't believe I've ever used it before, as a matter of fact." He adjusted his long stride to her much shorter one.

"I wouldn't recommend using it again," she remarked dryly.

"You're coming with me, aren't you?" Connor shrugged out of his suit coat and draped it over an arm. "To be truthful, I don't spend much time in the city, picking up women. Or for any other reason, for that matter."

He was wearing a white dress shirt that fit snugly over wide shoulders then tapered, tucked into slim-waisted trousers. Alex hadn't believed men that good looking actually existed, and here she was going for tea with one. One who had already seen her faint. She shook her head with amazement.

"So if you're not from the city, where *are* you from?" Small talk. Small talk was safe and not too revealing. She could handle niceties.

"I run a ranch about two hours northwest of here."

"Ah." Well, she certainly wouldn't have to worry about seeing him again after today. She'd be able to look back on it as a bizarre, fantastical dream. A knight in shining chaps.

She giggled, then clamped her mouth shut at his raised eyebrow. "Is this the place?" she asked, changing the subject.

"It is." He held the door—more good manners, it seemed, seated her at a table and went to get drinks.

The coffee shop was trendy and didn't seem to suit either of them. She pictured him more of a local diner type, drinking black coffee from a thick white mug while some middle-aged waitress named Sheila read the specials of the day. Despite his formal appearance today, she got the impression that he wasn't totally comfortable in a suit.

In moments he returned with two steaming mugs… one of peppermint tea and one with straight black coffee. The café didn't suit her much, either. She usually bought coffee from a vending machine or drank it thick and black from behind the bar, not that she'd been drinking much lately. Still, she was touched and surprised that he'd thought to get her something herbal in deference to her pregnancy.

"Thanks for the peppermint. It was thoughtful of you."

"I'll admit I asked the girl behind the counter for something un-caffeinated. And the peppermint might be, um, soothing."

He handed her something wrapped in waxed paper. "I got you a cookie, just in case your blood sugar was low."

Alex wondered how he knew so much about the biology of pregnancy as she unwrapped the long, dry biscotti and tried a nibble. It seemed safe. A sip of the peppermint tea confirmed it. "Thanks. I think we're good."

His shoulders relaxed. "I'm glad. I'd hate to have a repeat of earlier.

She laughed a bit. "You'll have to find another method for your next damsel in distress."

Connor sipped his coffee, sucking in his lips as the hot liquid burned. "You seemed to need it. Plus my grandmother would flay me alive if I didn't help a lady in need."

"I thought chivalry was dead."

"Not quite." His smile was thin. "And this way I can procrastinate."

"I beg your pardon?" She put down her mug and stared at him.

"I have a meeting this afternoon. I'd rather spend the afternoon shovelling... well, you get the idea. I'm simply not looking forward to it."

"Why?"

He avoided her prying eyes and stared out the window. "It's a long story." He turned back. "What about you? What are your plans for you and your baby?"

She took another long drink of tea to settle the anxiety brewing in her belly. "Our plans are pretty open. I'm working, for now. Trying to figure out what to do next. It's temporary."

"You're not from here. I can tell by your accent."

"No. Ottawa."

He smiled. "I thought I sensed a little Ontario," he teased. "But there are so many easterners here now that for all I knew you could have lived here for years."

"Three weeks, two days and twenty-two hours," she replied. "I'm working at the Pig's Whistle Pub for now." She needed to find something else. But her tips were good and she'd have a hard time finding a boss as accommodating as Pete had been.

He didn't have to answer for her to know what he was thinking. It was a dead-end job and hardly one she could support herself *and* a baby on. She knew right away she'd said too much.

His brow furrowed a little and she somehow felt she'd failed a test. Which was ridiculous. He didn't even know her, and they wouldn't meet again, so his opinion shouldn't matter at all. She was working on coming up with a solution. Just because she hadn't come up with one yet didn't mean she wouldn't. Heck, she'd been finding her way out of scrapes for years. This one was going to take a little more ingenuity, that was all.

It was time to end this whole meet and greet thing. She pushed away her tea. "Listen, thanks for helping this afternoon and for the tea. But I should get going."

She stood to leave and he rose, reaching into his pocket.

"Here," he offered, holding out a card. "If you need anything, call me."

"Why would I do that?"

His face flattened and he stepped back at her sharp tone. "I'd like to be of help if I can. I'm at Windover Ranch, just north of Sundre."

She had no idea where Sundre was and had no plan of discovering the wonders of Windover Ranch, so she figured there'd be no harm in responding to his solicitude by being polite. She tucked the small white card into her jeans pocket.

"Thanks for the offer. It was nice meeting you, Connor."

She held out her hand, and he took it firmly.

Her eyes darted up to his and locked.

Another time, another place. She lost herself momentarily in their chocolatey depths. Perhaps in different circumstances she might have wanted to get to know him better. It was just her luck that she'd fainted in front of the first hot guy she'd seen in a good long time.

And it was the height of irony to meet someone like him, when she was obviously unavailable. She was pretty sure that being pregnant with another man's child was probably number one on a guy's "not in this lifetime" list.

"Goodbye," she whispered, pulling her hand away from his grasp.

Her steps were hurried as she exited the shop, but she couldn't escape the gentle and understanding look he'd given her as she'd said goodbye.

CPSIA information can be obtained
at www.ICGtesting.com
Printed in the USA
BVHW070929070421
604343BV00005B/737